D1085823

MYSTERY OF THE EMERALDS

**Trixie
Belden**

Your TRIXIE BELDEN Library

Trixie Belden and the
MYSTERY OF THE EMERALDS

BY KATHRYN KENNY

Cover by Jack Wacker

GOLDEN PRESS
Western Publishing Company, Inc.
Racine, Wisconsin

CONTENTS

MYSTERY OF THE EMERALDS

"Rabbit! Rabbit!" · 1

TRIXIE BELDEN awoke slowly, to the sound of a summer rain beating against her window. She half opened her eyes, stretched her arms above her head, and then, catching sight of a large sign tied to the foot of her bed, yelled out, "Rabbit! Rabbit!" She bounced out of bed and ran out of her room and down the hall.

"I've finally done it!" she cried as she dashed into the large bedroom shared by two of her three brothers.

The oldest, Brian, responded by drawing the covers tightly over his head and turning thumpily toward the wall, but Mart, her almost-twin, sat up excitedly and demanded to know *what* she had done to cause all this rumpus at eight o'clock in the morning— enough rumpus, in fact, to wake up Bobby, who at this moment appeared in the doorway.

Trixie's blue eyes were sparkling as she picked up

her youngest brother and twirled him round and
round, and then, plunking herself down on Brian's
bed, she said, "Well, ever since I was Bobby's age
I've been trying to remember to say 'Rabbit! Rabbit!'
and make a wish, just before going to sleep on the
last night of the month. If you say it again in the
morning, before you've said any other word, your
wish comes true." Trixie laughed. "But when I'd remember to say the magic words at night, I'd always
say something else before I went to sleep or forget
them in the morning or something. This time I put
up a sign to remind me. Gleeps! I hope that doesn't
spoil the charm!"

"I must say you're the luckiest of girls," Mart said
in his most sarcastic voice, extending his hand to con-
gratulate his sister. "And what stupendous thing did
you wish for, Trix? That you'd pass English next
year?"

Brian, unable to sleep through all this talk, rolled
over, poked his head out from under the covers, and
said, "I bet I know what she wished for—another
mystery. You know she's never happy unless she has
some puzzle or other cooking."

Trixie's face sobered, and in a characteristic gesture she pushed back the short, sandy curls from her
forehead. "As a matter of fact, I *did* sort of wish for
some excitement." She sighed. "After Cobbett's
Island, Sleepyside seems—well, a little pallid."

"Wow! Look who's getting sophisticated," jeered
Mart. "Watch out, old girl, or you'll die of ennui."

He loved to use long or unusual words.

"What's 'ennui,' Trixie? Is it sumpin' like measles or chicken pox?" Bobby asked, his eyes wide as he scrambled up onto the bed beside his sister. "I don't want Trixie to die," he cried. "She's the only sister I got."

"Of course she's not going to die," Brian assured him softly. " 'Ennui' is just a fancy way of saying you're tired of doing the same old thing all the time."

The tears dried magically, a smile broke over Bobby's face, and he said, "Oh! That's what I get every morning when I have to eat my cereal!"

The call of "Breakfast, children," interrupted their laughter, and they dashed downstairs in their pajamas to the large, friendly kitchen, where Mrs. Belden was frying bacon and eggs on the old-fashioned stove.

Their father, who worked in the Sleepyside bank, put aside his paper as they came in and, looking over the top of his glasses, greeted each of them. Trixie planted a quick kiss on top of his head as she went past him to her place at the table.

The Beldens lived in a comfortable old white farmhouse, a few miles outside the Hudson River town of Sleepyside. It was called Crabapple Farm and had been in the Belden family for six generations. Although larger and grander houses had been built around the ancient homestead over the years, they loved Crabapple Farm with its orchards and gardens. Mrs. Belden never found it a chore to care for and

harvest the fruits and vegetables the place yielded,
and in the fall, her pantry shelves were loaded with
preserves, pickles, and jellies. Even though the boys
sometimes grumbled about having to take care of
the chickens, they freely admitted that the Belden
eggs were the biggest and best they had ever seen.
Trixie, who hated housework, sometimes complained,
too, about having to help with the dishes or the dusting, but once when her mother, pretending to be
serious, suggested that they sell the house and move
to an apartment, where the housekeeping might be
a little easier, Trixie nearly exploded. It was a long
time before she was again heard to say, "Do I *have*
to? You mean right *now?*"

Trixie's best friends, Honey Wheeler and her
adopted brother, Jim, lived a little farther up Glen
Road, in an impressive mansion on a huge estate.
The fact that the Wheelers' wealth allowed them a
staff of servants and every luxury never interfered
with the young people's close friendship. Honey and
Trixie had met soon after Mr. Wheeler bought Manor
House, with its stable of horses, game preserve, and
swimming pool, hoping it would benefit his somewhat sickly daughter. Honey's real name was Made-
leine, but no one ever called her that now, and no
one seemed to remember who first gave her the nick-
name. Everyone agreed, however, that it suited her
perfectly, for Honey was always as cheerful and
sweet as she was pretty.

After the two girls became friends, Honey somehow forgot her ill health. There just wasn't time to be sick, with all they found to do. Their first adventure had been helping Jim Frayne, who was running away from a cruel stepfather. It had ended with Jim's inheriting half a million dollars from an uncle, his only relative, and being adopted by the Wheelers.

"What are you all going to do this rainy day?" Mr. Belden inquired as he put on his raincoat and prepared to leave for work.

"Don't you worry about their not having anything to do," Mrs. Belden answered. "I've been waiting for just such a day as this to clean out the attic and the top of the barn."

"Oh, Moms! Not again," groaned Brian. "Why, we just cleaned the barn—let's see, when was it?"

"*Tempus fugit,* dear brother," Mart said cheerily. "It was at least four years ago, because I remember what a fuss I made when Moms wanted to throw out my magnificent collection of rocks."

"Will it take all day?" Trixie asked a bit impatiently. "We're supposed to have a meeting of the Bob-Whites this afternoon up at the clubhouse. The president of the Heart Association wrote and asked if we'd help with their White Elephant Sale, and we have to talk it over and see what we can do."

"Well, that's a coincidence," Mrs. Belden said, "because I thought if we cleaned out the attic and barn, we might find some things to donate to the sale."

Trixie was suddenly all smiles. "Gleeps, Moms,"

she cried, "what a perfectly spiffy idea! You can count on *all* the Bob-Whites to help!"

The Bob-Whites of the Glen was a secret club that Jim had organized soon after he came to live with the Wheelers. Although they were forever getting involved in some mystery, they also found time to be of help to others. There were now seven regular members in the club—the three Beldens, Honey and Jim, Dan Mangan, and Diana Lynch. Dan's part-time jobs and a heavy school program prevented him from joining in all of the Bob-Whites' adventures, but he went with the club whenever he could. Di, as she was called, lived close by in another large house. Her twin brothers and sisters were much younger than she, so she welcomed membership in the club, because it gave her a chance to be with people her own age. Di had always been considered the prettiest girl in the group, with her shoulder-length black hair, fair skin, and large violet eyes.

"I think I'll phone Honey and Di and tell them to check and see what they can collect at their houses, and then we'll all meet late this afternoon to see what needs mending or repairing," Trixie said, her enthusiasm for the project growing all the time.

"Come on, Mart," she continued, "you and Brian get dressed and do the barn, and Moms and I will tackle the attic."

"I was planning to fix the muffler on my car," Brian said. He was always fussing with his old jalopy, usually quite successfully, because he was a superb mechanic. "But the co-president of the Bob-Whites is issuing orders, so I guess the Queen of the Highways will have to wait. All set, Mart?"

"All set," Mart growled, "but let me tell you, Trixie Belden, one day is all I'm going to give up for any elephant, white or purple. So don't try to inveigle me into working all week on some old wrecked piece of furniture or something."

Mart and Trixie frequently appeared to be engaged in a running feud, but underneath they were very fond of each other. Their birthdays were less than a year apart, and, although Mart was taller than Trixie, they looked enough alike to be twins.

Trixie met her brother's statement with a chilly silence as she went off to the telephone.

"This promises to be a productive day," Mrs. Belden commented as she walked with her husband to the door and bade him good-bye. She didn't know, as she said it, just *how* productive it would turn out to be.

She gathered up several cartons from the porch and headed for the back stairs that led to the attic. She was soon joined by Trixie and Bobby, who announced, "I wanna hunt for the elephant, too."

"Where do you want me to start?" Trixie asked her mother as she pushed aside an enormous cobweb stretched between an old chest and a Victorian umbrella stand.

"Why don't you begin with that chest, dear? I haven't the faintest idea what's in it. As a matter of

fact, I don't think I've ever used it. It's probably full
of your great-grandmother's things. Take a look." Mrs.
Belden went on to sort out some discarded picture
frames on the other side of the attic.

Trixie opened the top drawer and took out two
little bonnets. The feathers were no longer perky,
and the ribbons were faded, but they were still
pretty. Trixie put one on and tied the ribbon under
her chin. She brushed the dust from the mirror over
the chest and surveyed herself critically. She was
surprised to find the image rather pleasing. Her
face, outlined by the soft lines of the bonnet, took
on an unaccustomed sweetness, and Trixie resolved
to try harder to curb her tomboy impulses. She forgot
the resolve a moment later.

Pushing the little bonnet back on her head, she
tried to open the drawer below, but it was stuck fast.
She braced her foot against the bottom of the chest
and gave a mighty tug. It worked all too well! The
drawer came out completely, cascading its contents
all over Trixie, who, losing her balance, crashed
into the wall behind her.

"Trixie, are you hurt?" cried her mother, running
over to help her up.

There was a smudge of dust on the end of Trixie's
nose, but she wasn't hurt. "I'm fine, but I've broken
this board to smithereens," she said, looking curiously
at the splintered wall behind her. "What's back there,
anyway?" she asked, pushing the board to one side.

"It's just a crawl space over the wing of the house

where the kitchen is," her mother answered. "It's too small to be of any use, so I guess it was just boarded up when the attic was finished off. It doesn't even have a window."

Trixie thought no more about it as she picked up the scattered clothing from the chest. The attic was getting very warm, and her forehead was beaded with perspiration.

"Speaking of windows, why don't we open this one and get a little air in here?" she suggested. "The rain won't blow in. It's coming straight down."

As she made her way to the dormer, she looked out and saw that the rain was actually letting up and the sun was trying to break through the clouds. She opened the window, and, as she turned to go back to her work, a streak of sunlight fell across the room and lanced through the broken board. Trixie caught a glimpse of something through the crack—a kind of dull metallic gleam. There was more than just an empty space back there, but what? She pushed and pulled the board impatiently until it came loose.

"Hey, Bobby, run and get the flashlight in my room, will you? There's something in there, but I can't make out what it is," she said, her voice suddenly tense with excitement.

"Sure, Trix, but wait for me. I wanna go in, too," begged Bobby as he good-naturedly went to get the light she wanted.

Mrs. Belden, who had come over to see what was going on, laughingly asked, "Now, what have you

unearthed this time?" She was no longer surprised
when Trixie uncovered a new mystery; it had happened so often before. In fact, she had even begun to
believe that Trixie's dream of starting a detective
agency with Honey wasn't as farfetched as it might
seem.

Before Trixie had time to answer, Bobby came
padding up the stairs. "Here's the light, Trixie. You
go first. I'm skeered!" he cried, fear crowding out his
curiosity. "There may be a ghost in there or sumpin'."
His eyes were wide, and he edged up to his mother's
side for reassurance.

Trixie squeezed through the opening into the
room, which was, indeed, little more than a crawl
space. On the floor was a pile of old clothing, which
she gingerly nudged with the toe of her sneaker. A
mouse scurried out from a coat sleeve and ran away
into the darkness. Trixie shivered, despite the stifling
heat, but since Bobby by now had got up nerve
enough to join her, she concealed her momentary
fright. Stooping, she picked up a round object that
lay on top of the old clothes.

"Gleeps, Bobby, this looks like Brian's old Boy
Scout canteen. How could it ever have got in here—
and where do you suppose these old clothes came
from?"

"I dunno, Trixie, but I don't like it in here. It's
spooky. Let's go back to Moms." Bobby caught
Trixie's hand and started pulling her toward the
opening in the wall.

"Okay, Bobby, you're a brave boy to come with me," Trixie said gently, permitting the little boy to lead her back to the main part of the attic.

Mrs. Belden hadn't the faintest idea where the old clothes and the canteen had come from. "That part of the house has been closed as long as I've lived here," she said. "Maybe your father will know something about it."

"This couldn't be Brian's canteen, then," mused Trixie as she examined it more closely. "No, this one is much heavier and older looking."

"You know, it looks like the kind the soldiers carried during the Civil War," Mrs. Belden said. "I remember my great-grandfather had one. He'd bring it out and let us children play with it."

"Do you think it would be worth any money at the White Elephant Sale?" Trixie asked. "It's nothing we can use."

"Well, someone might be interested in it as a collector's item. Personally, I'd rather have a nice clean Thermos bottle," Mrs. Belden answered, laughing. "And we might as well get rid of those old clothes, too. Hand them out to me, Trixie. I'll put them in this box, and we can burn them later."

"Jeepers, I hate to touch those dirty old things," Trixie said as she glanced around the attic. Her eye finally lighted on an old pair of tongs. "I know what! I'll use these and spare my lily-white hands."

She slipped back through the narrow opening into the crawl space. Out came an ancient overcoat,

followed by a worn blanket. As Trixie was picking up
a moth-riddled pair of pants, an envelope dropped
out of one of the pockets. She put it in her own
pocket, quickly deciding to open it later, in private.
It was probably of no importance, but she'd had
enough teasing lately about her playing detective.

On the other hand, she thought to herself, *it just
could be the beginning of something interesting.*

Mystery From the Past • 2

By FOUR O'CLOCK, Trixie and her mother decided to call it a day. Tired and disheveled, they went downstairs, carrying the boxes of articles they had sorted out for the sale—some china, a beautiful old parasol, a mirror, and odds and ends of clothing.

Trixie went out on the porch and called to her brothers to come in for a snack. Bobby, who had deserted the attic soon after lunch to go out to the barn with Mart and Brian, came running to the house, the case of an alarm clock in one hand and its works in the other, followed by Reddy, the Beldens' red Irish setter, who was never very far away from the little boy.

"I'm gonna fix this up good as new for the elephant sale," he announced proudly. "Mart's gonna show me how, aren't you, Mart?"

"I sure am, but right now I'm ready to tear into

those cookies. Wow! My favorite kind, too!" he cried
as he caught sight of a plate piled high with home-
made molasses cookies. He grabbed his mother and
spun her around the kitchen until she begged him
to let her go.

"Mart, you're making me dizzy!" She laughed as
she straightened her apron and pushed her hair back
into place. "Now, you all go and wash your hands
while I pour the milk. You look like hoboes."

"It's just good honest grime," Brian answered as
they went out to get cleaned up.

They were soon back, holding out their hands,
palms up, like three-year-olds.

"Do we pass inspection now, Moms?" Trixie asked
teasingly.

"I'll give you an 'A' for effort," Mrs. Belden replied,
"but I still see signs of cobwebs and dust in your
hair."

"Oh, don't worry about that," Trixie said. "I'll take
a quick shower as soon as we've finished eating, and
then, while Mart and Brian are getting cleaned up,
I'll go ahead and pick up Honey and Jim. Meet you
at the clubhouse in half an hour. Okay?"

"Sure, chief," Mart answered, helping himself to
another glass of milk.

"By the way," Brian said, "is the key still hidden in
the same place, Trix?"

"What did you say?" she asked, munching absent-
mindedly on a cookie. "I wasn't listening."

Brian repeated the question, wondering why his

sister was so preoccupied—and with what.

"So far as I know, it is," Trixie said. "Remember, we closed up just before we went to Cobbett's Island. The place will probably need a good airing out. Whoever gets there first, open all the windows." With this, she was off, leaving a half-eaten cookie on her plate.

"I wish I had that child's energy," Mrs. Belden sighed as she brushed the crumbs from the red-checked tablecloth.

"She's certainly got more pep than I have, after cleaning up that old barn," Mart commented, "but she's acting so funny and vague. I'll bet she's got something mysterious cooking in that silly old head of hers. I wonder what?"

Mart, of course, could not know about the letter Trixie had found, which by now had filled her mind with curiosity. As she was undressing, she took it from her pocket and had her first real look at it. It was addressed to Mrs. John Sunderland, The Homestead, Croton-on-Hudson. The paper was old and brittle, folded and held by a wax seal. Her first impulse was to read it right then and there, but she decided to save time and wait until she was on her way to Honey's house.

She quickly showered and put on a clean pair of shorts and a matching blue blouse. She took only long enough to run a comb through her short, curly hair, at the same time scowling into the mirror as she looked at her nose, which was peeling from a new sunburn. Then she set out for the Manor House.

As soon as she was out of sight of Crabapple Farm, Trixie opened the letter, being careful not to break the seal but only to pry it away from the paper. Before she had time to read it, she heard the sound of horses' hooves, and Honey and Jim came into view, calling to her as they rode down the lane toward her.

"It turned out to be such a marvelous day, we thought we'd give the horses some exercise," Honey said as she reined Starlight up beside Trixie. "They missed us while we were at Cobbett's Island. Starlight was so frisky, I could hardly hold her."

"Here, jump up behind me, and I'll give you a free ride to the club," Jim said as he offered Trixie a hand. "I think this noble steed can carry us both."

"I'm not so sure!" Trixie laughingly replied. "I'm full of Moms's cookies and gallons of milk, and I must weigh a ton. Besides, I want to show you something before we go on."

"A letter?" asked Honey, catching sight of the paper in Trixie's hand. "Who's it from?"

Jim and Honey dismounted, and, leaving the horses to graze along the roadside, they perched on the post-and-rail fence that surrounded the Wheeler estate.

"I found it this morning when Moms and I were cleaning out the attic, and I haven't had a chance to read it yet," Trixie said.

"In the *attic!*" Jim exclaimed. "Who's it from?"

"Hurry up! What are we waiting for?" Honey urged as Trixie unfolded the letter.

There were two pages, written in small but very legible script. At the top of the first sheet was an embossed crest, identical to the one imprinted in the wax. The words *Lux et Pax* underneath it, which had not been clear on the seal, were now easy to read.

"Sounds like a new kind of soap, doesn't it?" chuckled Trixie. "What does it mean, Jim?"

Jim, the oldest of the Bob-Whites, was an excellent student, and since Latin had been part of his college preparatory course, it was easy for him to translate the words.

"It means 'Light and Peace,'" he said. "I like that! It would make a good motto for my school, wouldn't it?" Jim's dream was to start a school for homeless boys when he finished college.

Trixie started reading:

> "'Rosewood Hall
> "'June 27th

"'Dearest Sister,

"'What an age it seems since your visit, when actually it has been less than a year. I started several times to talk to you while you were here about my deep concern over the growing dissension between the North and the South, but I could not bring myself to spoil the pleasure of your stay with unhappy thoughts. Since you left, my apprehension has increased daily. What may happen to Rosewood, my husband, and my child, no one knows, but my intuition tells me there is bound to be a long, hard struggle ahead.

" 'Because I am a Northerner, people here have always treated me with a certain coolness, as though I didn't really belong in Virginia. Did you sense that when you were here? I'm sure they didn't like the idea of one of their sons marrying a girl from the North, no matter how respectable her family. It was as though Lee had broken an unwritten law! I have many acquaintances here but not a single close friend in whom I can confide.

" 'The question of slavery is on everyone's lips. Fortunately, Lee and I are of the same opinion about this matter. We freed all the slaves here at Rosewood some time ago. Most of them did not want to leave the plantation, where they had spent all their lives, and so they stayed on, for either wages or a share of the crops. But on the other plantations, where their relationship with the owners is not so good, slaves have been escaping to the North in great numbers. Feelings are running high, and there is bound to be trouble soon.

" 'Reading between the lines of your letter, which finally reached me, I know that you are aware of the situation and what is being done about it. Hence my decision to write you about the emerald necklace. This afternoon I hid it, and, with Lee's consent and approval, I am sending Rufus, whom I'm sure you will remember, to you with this note. He has served this family since before Lee was born. Now he is old and not too well. We want to assure his well-being. He is leaving tomorrow with someone who will know the proper "lines" to take. His journey will be precarious, I know, and all we can do is hope and pray he reaches you safely. In case anything should happen to him en route, however, I am not divulging in this note where I have hidden the necklace. I have put directions for locating it in the place where we spent the last afternoon you were here.

" 'My heart is filled with sadness and a great desire to see you again, but my duty is with my family. Where will we all be next Christmas? Will one of us be able to wear the emeralds, or will their proverbial curse visit us if they are not worn on that day? I pray not, but time alone will tell.

" 'Your devoted sister,
" 'Ruth' "

There was dead silence as Trixie finished reading, and the three looked at one another with solemn faces. They slid off the fence and walked slowly up the road toward the grazing horses.

Finally Jim said, "Trix, you've hit upon something pretty mysterious and a little eerie, but it was so far away and so long ago that I don't see how you can ever hope to do anything about it."

"She'll find a way, Jim, if I know Trixie," Honey said, rising to her friend's defense, "and you can be sure every one of the Bob-Whites will help her—you included—until she does find a way."

"Oh, simmer down, Honey; you know I'll help her,"
Jim answered with a smile, "but how in heaven's
name can you go about unraveling a mystery as old
as this one?"

Trixie's brows were furrowed with thought as she
said, "I don't know *how*, Jim. I only know that I've
got to try."

They had been so preoccupied with the letter that
no one had noticed the minutes slipping by. Suddenly
Trixie looked at her wristwatch and cried, "Gleeps,
we'd better step on it. It's after four now. We'll have
to pay a fine for being late."

"Well, the club coffers need some replenishing, I
guess." Honey laughed. "I haven't paid my dues in
weeks."

The clubhouse originally had been the gatehouse
on the Wheeler estate. It had been unoccupied for
years and consequently in a very run-down condition when the Bob-Whites decided to use it for their
meetings. The boys had put on a new roof, floored
the interior, and partitioned one side for storage of
sports equipment—skis, skates, tennis rackets, and
camping gear. Honey, who sewed beautifully, had
made gay curtains for the windows, which, with the
simple furniture they had collected, made it a very
attractive room. They not only had many good times
here but had also planned several projects to help
those less fortunate than themselves.

Mart, Brian, and Diana were busy sweeping and

dusting when the others arrived. All but one of the windows were wide-open.

"Leave that one down, Trix," Brian warned his sister as she started toward it. "A robin has built her nest on the sill. Look; there are four very hungry babies in it, and Mr. and Mrs. Redbreast are being run ragged trying to fill them up."

"Just like people!" Mart said. "But how about getting started? Would our *late* president like to call the meeting to order? You were in an awful hurry a little while ago. What slowed you down, Sis?"

"If you'll all sit down, I'll tell you," Trixie said seriously. She took her place with Jim, the club's co-president, at the head of the table, the other Bob-Whites gathering quickly around, sensing that something unusual was in the wind.

Diana, looking pretty, as always, in a soft lavender dress that set off her dark hair and violet eyes, suggested that they skip the regular business of reading the minutes and roll call. "Let's hear what Trixie has to say," she urged, and everyone agreed.

They leaned forward expectantly as Trixie read the letter aloud. When she finished, she related how she had found it in the attic at Crabapple Farm. She was more explicit now about her discovery in the hidden compartment under the roof. "The letter fell out of a tattered pair of trousers I found in the little room. Moms doesn't know how they got there, and *I* can't even guess," she said, throwing up her hands in exasperation. "Unless—"

"Unless what, Trixie?" Honey asked breathlessly. "What do you think?"

"Remember last year when we were studying about the Civil War and slavery and secession and everything?" Trixie asked. "Well, isn't it possible that Rufus may have stopped at our house on his way to Croton, where Mrs. John Sunderland lived?"

"By Jove, I think you've got something there, Trix," Brian said. "He could have been hidden up there in the crawl space. Maybe our house was part of the Underground Railroad. Let's ask Dad about it when he gets home tonight."

It was inevitable that, with the letter on everyone's mind, the Bob-Whites found it difficult to get down to the business of the White Elephant Sale. But, after a good deal of speculation about the mystery of the hidden room, Trixie reminded them that they had to come to some decision about their list of contributions to the sale.

Before they adjourned, they had compiled quite a list of things to donate. "And why can't we offer to pick up articles from people who have no way of delivering their stuff?" suggested Mart.

"Good idea, and we might offer to help sell, too," Honey added.

After a vote was taken and everyone agreed to the plan, Trixie asked Di to write to the Heart Association, offering their services. Di was the quietest member of the group, and Trixie liked to give her things to do to make her feel that she was really an important member of the Bob-Whites.

As the meeting broke up, Trixie told Honey and Di that she would phone them later. "In the meantime, you all might be doing a little quiet research on the Underground Railroad, especially to see if it ever ran through Sleepyside."

"You talk as though you thought it was a real railroad," Mart said jestingly. "Do you think it was kind of like the New York subway system?"

"Of course not. I'm not quite such a lame-brain, dear brother, even if I'm not as brilliant as you." Trixie shot the words at him with a toss of her head and the color rising in her cheeks. She adored Mart, but sometimes his teasing got just the result he hoped for—it made her boiling mad!

Brian broke the mood. "I think we all agree," he said seriously, "that Trix has uncovered a real mystery—one that's really going to require everything we've got, if we're going to find the answer to it."

Trixie looked at her older brother gratefully. "Thank you, Brian," she said softly. "I know it looks hopeless right now, but"—she clenched her fist—"we've just got to try!"

The First Step · 3

BOBBY WAS HELPING Mrs. Belden shell peas on the back porch when his brothers and sister returned. Mart grabbed a handful from the bowl on his mother's lap as he went past.

"Go easy, Mart, these are the first of the season, and there aren't too many big enough to pick yet," she admonished him.

"I know," said Mart, grinning. "That's why I helped myself. I remember last year I got cheated."

"That'll be the day, when *you* don't get enough to eat," Trixie said. "Is Dad home yet, Moms?"

"No, but he should be here any minute now. Reddy's nose is beginning to quiver, and that's always a sure sign your father's coming. I do believe that dog knows exactly when he leaves his office," Mrs. Belden said.

"He'd make a wonderful hunting dog, but I'm glad

we never trained him for that," Brian commented. "I like to think of the woods creatures living without fear of man or dog."

"Reddy hasn't been trained to do anything, but the old boy is faithful," Mart said. "I don't think he'd let anyone get near Bobby if we weren't here. And remember how he came for help when we were lost in the blizzard?"

Reddy sensed that he was being praised, and his tail thumped the floor in appreciation. Suddenly he let out a big woof, leaped off the porch, and raced up the driveway. Almost immediately, the Belden station wagon turned into the yard, and Mr. Belden got out.

"Hello, everybody! Is dinner ready? I'm starved!" he called out as he came up the porch steps, lifting Bobby and kissing him.

Bobby wiped his cheek on his sleeve as he mumbled, "I'm too big to get kissed. You don't kiss Mart and Brian. Only girls get kissed. I'm a big boy now."

"Okay, Bobby." His father laughed. "I'll kiss two of the prettiest girls in Sleepyside—that is, if they have my dinner ready."

"Coming up, sir," Trixie answered, bowing low, then following her mother into the house to help set the table.

It was not long before the family was seated around the big kitchen table, where they preferred to eat most of their meals. After everyone had been served the roast lamb, mashed potatoes, and peas,

Trixie turned to her father and, trying to make her voice sound casual, said, "Dad, have you any idea how an old canteen and some other stuff got up in that space over the kitchen?"

"What space over the kitchen, Trix?" her father asked, obviously puzzled by her question.

"Well, I sort of backed into it today." Trixie giggled as she thought how ridiculous she must have looked —sitting on the floor, with a drawer full of clothes on top of her and that old bonnet on her head. "While Moms and I were up in the attic, I was trying to get a drawer open, and I fell and broke into a funny little space, and there was this canteen—"

"This canteen? *What* canteen, Trixie?" Mr. Belden interrupted.

"Oh," Trixie laughed ruefully. "I'm going too fast, as usual. I'll start at the beginning and go get it— the canteen, I mean."

She sprang up from the table and ran out of the room, returning a moment later with the old canteen. Mr. Belden laid down his fork, pushed himself back from the table, and took it in his hands.

"Hmmm, that's an old one, all right," he said as he turned it over and over. "I'm sure I don't know about the room over the kitchen or how this got in it, but I'll take a look at it after dinner."

"Couldn't you come up now and see it?" Trixie urged.

"And miss your mother's chocolate cake? We'll go up as soon as we've finished eating," he promised.

Trixie managed to control her excitement and ate two pieces of cake herself before she got the flashlight and, followed by her father, Mart, and Brian, went up to the attic.

Mr. Belden crawled through the broken board and examined every corner of the hidden room. He found that Trixie hadn't overlooked a single thing. There was nothing there now except cobwebs and the dust of years.

"What do you think, Dad? Could it have been a secret hideaway?" Trixie asked.

"Yes, it *could* have been," Mr. Belden answered slowly. "You know, while I was in there, something began to come back to me, something my grandfather used to talk about when I was a little boy. I'd forgotten all about it until now."

"Jeepers, Dad, you've just got to remember!" Trixie cried. "Think hard!"

"Why all the interest in an old canteen, Trixie?" he asked, looking at her quizzically.

"Oh, I suppose she thinks if she rubs it hard, like Aladdin's lamp, a mystery may pop out of it," Mart teased.

Trixie was grateful to her brother for emphasizing her interest in the canteen, because she didn't want anyone but the Bob-Whites to know about the letter, at least not until she had had more time to investigate it.

"I guess I'm turning into a Civil War fan." Trixie laughed. "Tell me what your grandfather said, Dad."

"Well, when I was about Bobby's age, I used to love to climb up on his lap. He had a fascinating gadget on the end of his gold watch chain, and while he talked to me, he'd take it out of his pocket and clean his pipe with a little silver spoon and scraper, and then, after he'd fill the pipe with wonderful, sweet-smelling tobacco, he'd press it down with the little tamper and light it. I was more interested in watching this ritual than in hearing about a war I wasn't old enough to understand. I vaguely recall, however, his telling me about slaves coming to this house for refuge and being hidden during the day and going away secretly at night, and I seem to remember one in particular who was nursed by my great-grandmother when he fell ill."

"Do you know what happened to him?" Brian asked.

"I don't remember," Mr. Belden answered, frowning as he tried to recall the end of the story. "Maybe it'll come back to me later. It all happened before my great-grandfather went off to the Civil War."

Trixie was fascinated. Crabapple Farm *must* have been a stop on the Underground Railroad! She spent the rest of the evening looking among her father's books for any that might have something on the subject. One of them described the system in some detail—how the houses where people were hidden were called "stations," the various routes were called "lines," and those who were passed along were referred to as "packages" or "freight." Trixie remembered the use of the word "lines" in the letter she had found and how the writer had put it in quotation marks. *Surely*, Trixie thought to herself, *she must have meant that Rufus was being sent north along the Underground.* She decided to go the next morning to the Sleepyside library. Maybe there she could find something more about the actual routes and discover if any ran up the Hudson Valley. She called Honey and Di to tell them about her father's half-remembered story and to ask them to go with her. Di couldn't because she had to go to New York with her mother, but Honey was free, and they made a date to meet at ten the following day.

Trixie had just finished helping her mother with the dusting next morning, when she heard Honey at their back door.

"Am I ever glad to see you—and fifteen minutes early, too!" Trixie exclaimed, coming out on the porch and shaking the dustcloth with savage vigor. "I hate dishwashing, I hate to make beds, and, most of all, I hate to dust!"

"Oh, it's not as bad as all that, is it, Trix?" Honey asked.

"Not really, I guess," Trixie sighed. "It's just that it seems to interfere with my 'detecating,' as Bobby would say."

"Well, hurry up and take off that silly apron. It doesn't make you look one bit more domestic." Honey laughed, pulling at the tie.

As the two friends rode off toward town on their bikes, Trixie suddenly asked, "Do you know anyone in Croton-on-Hudson, Honey?"

"No," Honey replied. "The only time I've ever been there was when Sleepyside played basketball with them last year and Jim took me along. Why?"

"Oh, I was just thinking about Mrs. Sunderland, to whom that letter was addressed. Do you suppose there are any Sunderlands left who still live anywhere near there?" Trixie mused.

"You know, the telephone book stood us in good stead when we were looking for Mrs. Hall down at Cobbett's Island. Have you thought of trying it again?" Honey asked.

"I'm afraid it's such an obvious thing to do that I just plain didn't think of it, dear partner." Trixie laughed. "Let's look as soon as we get to Mr. Lytell's store. But," she warned, "try to act perfectly natural when we go in, and don't discuss anything until we get outside. Remember how snoopy he was when Jim was hiding out in the old Mansion."

Fortunately, Mr. Lytell was waiting on a customer when the girls entered, and they went to the back of the store, where the telephone directories were chained to the wall. Mr. Lytell wasn't going to run the risk of anyone's stealing them, even though they were not really his property.

Trixie, trying to look casual, thumbed through the book until she came to the S's. There was only one Sunderland in Croton, a Miss Julie, living on Revolutionary Road. Trixie pointed it out to Honey, and then, seeing Mr. Lytell looking at them over his glasses, she went into the booth and pretended to make a call.

"Phone out of order up at your house?" the old gentleman asked Trixie as she and Honey came up to the front of the store a few minutes later.

"No, Mr. Lytell, there's nothing at all wrong with it," Trixie answered with a saccharine smile. Then she and Honey went out, leaving Mr. Lytell's curiosity completely unsatisfied.

"You're improving, Trixie. You know, you didn't blush even a little bit," Honey said warmly. "Now, what's the next step?"

Trixie looked at her wristwatch, and then, after a moment, she answered, "Why don't we bike up to Croton, take a look at Revolutionary Road, and see if we can find where Miss Julie lives? We can go to the library tonight."

"That's a wonderful idea! Croton's only a few miles from Sleepyside, and the exercise will do us good," Honey answered. "We'll stop at Wimpy's Diner and get some sandwiches to eat along the way."

"And we'd better make an honest-to-goodness phone call, too, so our parents will know where we are," Trixie said as they pedaled off down the road.

As the girls approached Croton, they stopped at a gas station to inquire the way to Revolutionary Road.

"Why, that's way up by the reservoir," the station

attendant told them. "You'll walk more than ride
going up, but it'll be a breeze coming back," he added
good-naturedly. "Just follow this road up the hill,
and bear left through the upper village until you
come to the dam. You can cross right over the top
of it, and Revolutionary Road will be the first on your
left."

"Oh, I remember now!" Trixie cried. "There's a
lovely park under the dam, with a fountain. We went
there once for a picnic. It'll be a perfect place to eat
our lunch."

"If we ever get there," Honey moaned. "I'm ex-
hausted already."

"You'll get your second wind soon," Trixie en-
couraged her. "We can't turn back now."

"I've already used up my second wind and my
third, but maybe I'll catch my fourth before it's too
late," Honey said as she pushed the hair off her forehead.

Even though they were anxious to explore Revolutionary Road, the girls took a long time to eat their
lunch. It was a wonderful day. The water poured
over the spillway at one side of the dam, making
miniature rainbows where the sun hit the spray. They
stretched out on the cool grass and watched the
clouds laze across an incredibly blue sky, until they
both felt revived and ready to pedal on their way.

They had not gone far along Revolutionary Road
before they rounded a curve and saw ahead of them
a small but lovely old house. It was nestled at the

foot of a hill, as though seeking protection from the weather. The gray shingled roof sloped in a gentle curve over a wide veranda. At the side of the house was an ivy-covered well with a bucket hanging above it.

"I'm dying of thirst," Trixie said. "Do you suppose it would be all right to take a drink?"

Before Honey had time to answer, the girls saw the side door of the house open. A frail-looking, white-haired old lady came out and down the path to the gate.

"I saw you young people from my upstairs window and thought you looked rather hot and tired. Wouldn't you like a drink of my wonderful well water?" she asked as she approached them.

"We were just wondering if it would be all right for us to have a drink. We *are* thirsty after our ride," Trixie answered.

"You wait right here, and I'll fetch some glasses," the old lady said. "By the way, let me introduce myself. I'm Miss Sunderland."

Miss Sunderland! It was all Trixie could do to contain her excitement. Darting a warning glance at Honey, she said, scarcely breathing, "I—I've heard your name, Miss Sunderland— I think your house is called The Homestead, isn't it?"

"Indeed it is, my dear," the old lady answered briskly.

Trixie and Honey glanced at each other swiftly, their eyes shining. Then, struggling not to show her excitement, Trixie introduced Honey and herself.

"We're from Sleepyside," she added. "It was such a nice day, we decided to picnic by the dam and— Revolutionary Road is beautiful. Does it really date back that far?"

"Oh, my, yes!" Miss Sunderland answered with a smile. "You let the bucket down while I get some glasses, and then I'll tell you all about it—and about this house, too."

"Isn't she adorable?" Honey whispered as the old lady left them. "Are you going to tell her about the letter?"

"I don't know yet." Trixie was almost breathless. "Let's wait and see what she has to say. Maybe we should just try to get some leads today and wait until later to tell her— Shh! Here she comes!"

"I thought you might like some fruit, too," Miss Sunderland said as she returned. She was carrying a basket of beautiful ripe fruit and two glasses. She filled the glasses with water from the mossy bucket and invited the girls to sit down and relax.

"Now, you were asking about this road," Miss Sunderland said. She sat down in a comfortable wicker chair alongside the well, smoothed her neat print dress, and folded her hands in her lap. "Did you notice that it isn't even paved? Well, it never has been. There aren't many cars come through this way. It's much too winding. It's just the way it was years and years ago, and most of the houses go way back, too."

"Have you lived here long?" Trixie asked.

"Oh, yes, my dear, I've lived here all my life, and I'll be—let me see, how old will I be?" Miss Sunderland paused, her brows wrinkling as she tried to recall her age. "I guess I'll be eighty-nine my next birthday —or is it ninety? My memory isn't as good as it used to be." She laughed. "Why, I even forgot where I put my gloves yesterday, but I finally found them, and do you know where? In the refrigerator, of all places!" She chuckled softly as she thought about it.

"Do you live here all alone?" Honey's question was solicitous. She couldn't help feeling that Miss Sunderland's advanced years and obvious absentmindedness made it a bit dangerous for her to be by herself.

"Well, yes and no," Miss Sunderland answered ambiguously. "You see, I have Neil to run errands for me and look after the place. He's a nice boy, too," she added, nodding her head to emphasize the point. "He just happened along one day, wanting work, and I took him in. He has a couple of rooms over the barn, where the hired man used to live, and he helps out on a farm down the road a piece. He just went down there to get some milk and eggs for me. He should be back pretty soon. And my neighbor stops by every day to check on me, as though I needed checking at my age." She chuckled. "And the first of the month, I get the money from the bank. I am, as you might say, comfortably off." Her blue eyes twinkled.

"And you have no relatives?" Trixie pursued.

"No, not a single one that I know of. My parents died when I was just a young thing. I wasn't born until quite a while after my father came back from the Civil War. My only relative was an aunt, whom I never saw. Seems to me she went south. Yes, I'm sure she did. Ruth went south and got married. Never did come back home."

"Here It Is!" • 4

TRIXIE and HONEY were spellbound. This must be the aunt who had written the letter from Virginia! Would Miss Julie have any more information about what happened to Ruth, whom she had never seen and who, so long ago, had gone away from home? Was this the end of the trail or just the beginning? The next few minutes would probably give the answer.

With bated breath, Trixie asked, "Why do you think Ruth left such a lovely place as this, Miss Sunderland?"

There was a long pause. The old lady twirled her thumbs as she looked off across the meadow, seeming to forget for the moment that the girls were there. Finally, with a little shake of her head, she said, "I suppose it was what makes lots of young folks leave home. She probably fell in love with some young man— Yes, I remember Mother saying she married

49

and went off to Virginia when she was little more than a girl."

"And then?" Trixie's question was almost a whisper as she tried to encourage Miss Sunderland to reminisce further.

"Well, let me see," she said slowly. "Seems to me Ruth had a baby—she would be my cousin, wouldn't she? Then later, Ruth died after her husband was killed in the war. My goodness, what a long time ago that was. I don't see why you young folks are interested in all this. I'm afraid I've been talking too much again." She laughed as she brought her attention back to the girls.

Trixie glanced at Honey as if to ask her if she felt the time was right to mention the letter. When she saw Honey give an imperceptible nod, Trixie said, "As a matter of fact, we are very interested, Miss Sunderland, because yesterday I found a letter up in our attic. I think your Aunt Ruth wrote it."

"A letter in *your* attic? But how could that be?" Miss Sunderland asked, edging her chair up closer to Trixie.

Very slowly, and as gently as possible, Trixie told about Rufus and the necklace. There was a long pause. Miss Sunderland was lost in thought again, trying to comprehend it all and fit the pieces together.

"What a strange story!" she finally said. "That girl must have had a lively imagination, just like my mother. She was always making up stories for me when I was a little girl. An emerald necklace! Imagine!"

"You mean you don't think it's true—about Rufus and all?" Trixie asked.

"Maybe it is and maybe it isn't." Miss Sunderland's eyes twinkled. "But one thing I know: I'm much too old to care about emeralds. Never did like anything except plain gold jewelry, and not much of that, either."

"You said, 'Maybe it is,' Miss Sunderland," Trixie said. "Would you mind if we tried to find out more about it?"

"Mercy, no, child," the old lady answered warmly. "I know how young folks like to dream. You just go right ahead and see if you can find the necklace. A charmed one, too, they say. Hmm."

"One more question, and then we should be on our way," Trixie continued. "Have you any idea where Rosewood Hall was? That's where the letter was written from, so that part must be real."

"Rosewood Hall, Rosewood Hall," Miss Sunderland mused. "No, I don't rightly think I do, although the name has a faintly familiar sound. I wonder—"

Trixie and Honey kept perfectly still, waiting for whatever it was the old lady was groping for.

"No, I don't recall anything about Rosewood Hall, but maybe you'd find some mention of it in my father's diaries. He kept them for several years, and I have them all," she volunteered.

"Oh, may we look at them?" Honey and Trixie

asked almost in the same breath.

At that moment they saw a young man coming up the road.

"Hi, Miss Julie," he called out cheerily as he jumped over the fence, carefully balancing an old-fashioned milk can in one hand and a basket of eggs in the other.

"Why, it's Neil," Miss Sunderland said pleasurably.

The boy was tall and rangy, with wide shoulders and slim hips. His light brown hair was carefully combed—almost too carefully, Trixie thought to herself. His blue jeans and T-shirt were clean but worn, and his scuffed cowboy boots looked more than a bit incongruous.

When Miss Sunderland introduced Trixie and Honey, Neil gave them an appraising look and said, "Pleased to meetcha. Don't think I've seen you around these parts before." He had set the milk and eggs on the edge of the well, and, as he spoke, he stuck his thumbs into the pockets of his jeans.

"No, we're from Sleepyside," Trixie answered a bit coolly and then added, "and where do *you* come from?"

There was a hint of sarcasm in her voice, for she had taken an immediate dislike— No, "dislike" wasn't the word for it. She just had a feeling that Neil was a little fresh. He reminded her vaguely of Dan Mangan when she first met him, although Neil was not as sullen as Dan had been.

"Oh, up north of here," Neil answered vaguely.

"I'm figuring on moseying down Texas way before winter and getting me a job on a ranch, but I took a fancy to Miss Julie here, so I'm stopping off for a while," he continued, giving the old lady an ingratiating smile.

The way he talks makes me feel he's read too many Western comic books, Trixie thought to herself. *I'd like to see him on a bucking horse. I bet he wouldn't last long!* Then, aloud, she said, "Well, that sounds like fun. No school, no worries."

"I'll say no more school!" Neil answered emphatically. "I hate school! Do you think they teach you anything about horses? No, just a lot of junk that don't do a guy no good."

A little grammar *might have done* you *some good,* Trixie felt like saying, but she controlled the impulse.

"Oh, do you like horses?" Honey asked brightly. "Trixie and I love to ride. We have several horses at home."

"I'll just bet you do, miss," Neil replied out of the corner of his mouth. "You see, I ain't that lucky, but I'll have me some horses one of these days, you can bet." With that, he picked up the milk and eggs and took them into the house.

"Isn't he a nice boy?" Miss Sunderland asked warmly. "See how he took those things to the kitchen without even being asked? I don't know how I'll ever get along without him."

"Well, he *does* seem to take good care of you," Trixie replied. "But isn't it too bad he left school so soon? He may need some more education."

"Oh, he'll turn out all right," Miss Sunderland said. "He's a bright boy, really, but he doesn't seem to have any roots, and all he can think about is horses."

"Well, I *hope* you're right," Trixie said dubiously, and then, realizing that it was getting late, she asked Miss Sunderland if it would be convenient for her to get the diaries before they left.

"What diaries?" the old lady asked, her misty blue eyes wide.

Trixie's heart sank as she gently reminded Miss Sunderland of her father's diaries and of Rosewood Hall.

"Oh, of course, of course. I got to thinking about something else there for a minute. I'll get them. They're right in his desk, where he always kept them." She pushed herself out of the chair and walked slowly toward the house.

While she was gone, Trixie and Honey compared notes on their impressions of Neil, and both admitted to some mental reservations about him. Trixie had the feeling that he was putting on an act, and she wondered why.

"Let's suggest to Miss Sunderland that this business of the letter be a secret among the three of us," Trixie said. "Do you think she'll agree?"

"Yes, but, after all, she's *ninety!* All we can do is hope. Her mind is really very fuzzy, isn't it?" Honey replied slowly.

"I guess you'd be fuzzy, too, if you'd lived that

long," Trixie said. "Shh! Here she comes, and, thank goodness, she has the diaries!"

"Now, my dears, you just take these along with you. I've heard of your family, Trixie. I guess there have been Beldens in Sleepyside for about as long as our family has been here in Croton. When you've finished with them, you can bring them back, and we'll have another nice visit." She handed the little leather journals to Trixie. They were tied together with faded red tape, the kind Trixie had seen on old legal documents her father had occasionally brought home from the bank. He had told her this was why people said any involved business was "all tied up in red tape."

"We'll take good care of them," Trixie assured her as she and Honey made their farewells. "We're going to keep the diaries and the letter a secret, Miss Sunderland, so you don't have to worry about a thing. *You* won't tell anyone, either, will you?" Trixie urged.

"Oh, no, it will be our little secret, won't it?" the old lady said, clasping her thin hands together gleefully. "I always loved having a secret!"

Trixie and Honey waved good-bye as they pedaled out of the gate and down the road, the diaries carefully packed in Trixie's bicycle basket. As soon as they had crossed the dam, they found that what the garage man had told them was certainly true. They flew down the hill, through the upper village, and onto the main road toward Sleepyside in no time at all. It was only when their speed slackened that they

had time to talk about the happenings of the afternoon.

"What do you make of it all? Do you think she will
be able to keep the letter a secret?" Honey asked.

"Jeepers, I don't know. She's so forgetful, she may
not even think about it once we're out of sight,"
Trixie answered. "On the other hand, who knows
how her mind will work?"

"I can't wait to get at the diaries," Honey said.
"When do you think we can start reading them?"

"We were going to the library tonight, remember?"
Trixie asked. "But now I think these are more important. Why don't you spend the night with me, and
we can work on them after dinner?"

"Wonderful! I'm starved, and your mother always
has such yummy food," Honey replied. "I'm sure
Miss Trask will let me stay."

Miss Trask, who had been one of Honey's teachers
when she was in private school, had come to stay
at the Manor House, first as governess and then,
when Honey had entered public school, as manager
of the household during Mr. and Mrs. Wheeler's
frequent absences. All the Bob-Whites adored her,
and she was always ready to help them with any of
their plans when they needed her.

The girls stopped off at Crabapple Farm to ask
Mrs. Belden if it was all right for Honey to eat dinner
there and spend the night.

"I'd be delighted to have you, Honey," Trixie's
mother said to her. "You know you're always wel-

come," she added with a smile, "especially tonight. Mart and Brian just told me Chuck Altemus wants them to come to his house. They're planning an overnight camping trip, so that leaves me with several extra pieces of fried chicken."

"*That's* what smells so good!" Honey exclaimed. "I'll hurry up to the house, get into something fresh, and be right back, Trixie."

By the time Trixie had set the table, showered, and changed her clothes, Mr. Belden was home from the bank, and Bobby, who'd had to amuse himself all day, was teasing for someone to read him a story.

"You pick out the story you want, and I'll read it to you," Honey, who had just come in, told him. "That is, if we have time before dinner," she added, looking toward Mrs. Belden.

"You'll have about ten minutes while the rice cooks," she answered.

"I wanna read about Jack 'n' the beanstalk," Bobby announced, climbing into Honey's lap with his book.

At dinner Trixie tried to hide her impatience. She could scarcely wait to get at the diaries, but she exerted all her self-control and chatted amiably through the meal about the trip to the dam and their picnic lunch. Honey started to help with the dishes after dinner, but Mrs. Belden said, "Thank you, dear, for offering, but I'll give you and Trixie a vacation tonight. I have a feeling you two have something important to discuss, so run along."

Trixie gave her mother a warm hug, and then she

and Honey went upstairs to Trixie's bedroom.

"Hurry, Trixie; untie the tape, and pray we'll find something that will give us some leads," Honey cried as the two curled up on the window seat.

There were twelve of the little books, all bound alike in soft brown leather. The pages were edged in gold, and each was divided into spaces for three days' entries.

"Here, Honey, you take the first one. Let's see—it's for the year 1859," Trixie said as she glanced inside.

The girls read in silence for a long time, then suddenly Honey burst out, "Trix, listen! I'm up to June, and here he begins to talk about his wedding and how he's packing up to move to The Homestead. 'Only five more days before Helen becomes Mrs. John Sunderland. Worked all day getting things in order for the move. The farm will need a lot of work on it after lying idle for two years.'"

"Oh, Honey, the pieces are beginning to fall into place. Now, if only we can find out something about Ruth. I haven't read anything important in 1860 yet. It's all about what crops he put in and how many chickens were hatched—all about the farm. I'm not going to skip any, though, because maybe something will turn up. We'll just have to keep on reading and hoping." Trixie again buried her nose in the book.

It was she who next broke the silence. "Gleeps, Honey! Here it is! 'Leaving tomorrow for Cliveden to visit Ruth and her husband at Rosewood. Hay all cut, and a slack time ahead for a few weeks,' and it's dated July fifteenth. We're getting someplace!"

"Cliveden! Do you suppose that's in Virginia?" Honey asked. "Miss Julie said Ruth had married and gone to Virginia. Where's your old geography book? We'll look it up."

Trixie rummaged around in her closet until she found the book. Then, with Honey looking over her shoulder, she searched until she found Cliveden on the map.

"There it is—that little bitty dot right there, where the James River begins to get wider. Whoopee!" Trixie cried. "We've found it!"

"Wait a minute, Trix," Honey said soberly. "I don't want to pour cold water on your discovery. It's great, but have you happened to think of where we go from here? Virginia is a long, long way from Sleepyside, you know."

"Oh, I hadn't thought of that," Trixie answered, her spirits quickly deflating. "Virginia! Rosewood Hall might just as well be in Outer Mongolia. Oh, Honey, what are we going to do?"

Di's Great Idea • 5

NEITHER OF THE GIRLS had much to say as they undressed for bed. They were such close friends that they sensed each other's moods, and Honey knew that Trixie felt terribly frustrated right now. She also knew that, given a little time, she would probably come up with some solution. She always had in the past. Things had a way of working out for her. Honey slipped into her dainty blue nightgown and matching robe and went off to brush her teeth. When she returned, Trixie, still with one shoe on, was sitting on the edge of the bed, her chin cupped in her hands.

"Honey," she said slowly, "I'll simply die if I can't explore this thing further. I just *know* that necklace is still hidden somewhere around Rosewood, and I've got to find it. Now, listen. Do you think the Bob-Whites would let us use the money in the treasury to go down to Virginia and see what we could find out?"

"Not so fast, Trixie," Honey answered as she sat down on the bed and put her arm around Trixie's shoulders. "In the first place, you know our parents wouldn't let us go off by ourselves. We'd have to have someone to drive us around, too, and do you realize how much it would cost and how little we have left in the treasury?"

"Wham! I just came in for a perfect landing! I'm right back on *terra firma* again." Trixie laughed. "I *knew* it was a wild idea. Maybe when Mart and Brian get home tomorrow, the Bob-Whites can have another meeting and talk it over. I'm too dead to think about it any more tonight. I'm not making any sense." She finished undressing, brushed her teeth, then threw herself into bed and blew a goodnight kiss to Honey.

She *thought* she wouldn't think about it any more, but she found that, tired though she was, her mind was spinning like a top. *I wish I could be like her,* she thought as she listened to Honey's even breathing and knew she was already fast asleep. She heard the old grandfather's clock in the hall strike ten, but she was still wide-awake. Something told her that she and Honey should have read further in John Sunderland's diary. They had been so excited about finding the location of Rosewood that they hadn't thought to go on.

Very quietly, so she wouldn't disturb Honey, Trixie

slid out of bed and, lifting up the top of the window
seat, got the diaries from the chest underneath, where
they had hidden them. Although the moon was high,
it wasn't bright enough to read by, so Trixie got out
the little flashlight that had been in her Christmas
stocking the year before. She found the entry about
the trip to Virginia and continued reading. The next
few entries told of the long train ride to the village
of Cliveden, of the arrival at Rosewood Hall, and of
their cordial welcome by Ruth and her husband.
Then came several entries about the plantation, with
comments about the differences in farming methods.

Jeepers! Trixie thought to herself. *This may have
been interesting to John, but it sure doesn't help me.
What were Ruth and Helen doing while their hus-
bands were riding around the plantation?*

She read through several more pages, and then her
eye caught sight of the two names she had been
watching for: "Plan to leave tomorrow for home.
Ruth and Helen spent the afternoon looking through
the old family burying ground, while Lee and I
visited the neighboring plantation."

Trixie's heart was in a turmoil! She started to wake
Honey and tell her about the discovery, but she
decided to wait until morning. Honey looked too
comfortable to be disturbed. By the time the clock
struck eleven, Trixie was finally asleep.

Mrs. Belden had left early the next morning for a
day in town with her husband and Bobby. The girls

were making toast and hot chocolate for their breakfast and talking about Trixie's discovery of the night before, when Mart and Brian burst in, wet and disheveled, from their sleep-out.

"Honey, you're a sight for my inflamed optics," Mart cried. "Now I can hope for a piece of toast that isn't charred á la Trixie, and while you're on your feet, you might scramble me an egg or two or three," he added as he patted Honey on the head and ran up to change his clothes.

"What happened to you two?" Trixie asked Brian. "An early morning swim with all your clothes on?"

"Don't tell me you didn't hear the thunderstorm around six this morning," he answered. "We had just got up and were building a fire when it hit us. By the time we got everything under cover in the pup tent, we were soaked, so we called it a day, packed up, and came home. See you in a jiffy, and you'd better make that scrambled-egg order a double! Double up on the toast, too."

"Those boys! Are they always hungry?" Honey asked good-naturedly as she got the eggs out of the refrigerator and broke them cleanly into a bowl. Honey loved to cook but didn't often have a chance at the Manor House. "Here, Trix, you fry some bacon."

"After that crack of Mart's, I'm not so sure I want to cook anything," Trixie said with a chuckle, "but I guess I can't get out of it that easily. Okay, here goes! But don't blame me if it burns," she added as she put several slices of bacon into the iron frying pan.

With Honey to keep an eye on things, the breakfast turned out very well. While they were eating,
Trixie told the boys about their expedition the
previous day and what they had found in the diaries.

"Whew! The plot thickens!" Mart whispered, pulling an imaginary cloak around his shoulders. "What's
the next move, Trixie, dear?"

"The next move is to talk with all the Bob-Whites
and see if someone is bright enough to figure out a
way for us to get to Virginia," Trixie said. "My brain
is incapable of producing one sensible suggestion."

"If the Queen only had a muffler, I might drive you
down," Brian offered.

"The Queen not only doesn't have a muffler, but
also, the last time I visited Her Excellency, she didn't
even have a backseat!" Trixie teased. "Thanks for
the offer, but I think we'll have to come up with a
better plan than that."

"Let's all meet at the club right after lunch. Maybe
by then someone will have had a cerebral tempest,"
Mart said.

"Sounds as though you've been reading some of
my medical books," Brian, who planned to become a
doctor, quipped. "What the dear lad is trying to
say is 'brainstorm.'"

"Just for *that* you can do the dishes," Trixie flung
at Mart. "Honey, will you call Di and Jim about the
meeting?" she asked. "I've just got to weed the aspar-
agus bed for Moms before she gets back. I promised

to do it when I first got home." She dashed out to the garden.

It was such a lovely day that the Bob-Whites decided to have their meeting outside the clubhouse, under a nearby weeping willow tree. Its graceful branches, reaching almost to the ground, made a kind of natural outdoor living room. Di was late, and while they were waiting for her, Jim amused them by feeding his pet catbird, Cheerio. Jim was a great lover of nature and had a special talent for winning the confidence of wild creatures. When Trixie commented on this, Jim laughed and said, "It doesn't take any talent to tame a catbird. They practically force their friendship on you. Cheerio followed me all the way from the house."

As though to prove what Jim had said, the gray bird gave a loud meow, perched on Jim's shoulder, and took a piece of dried doughnut from his lips.

Di soon joined them, and although she said she'd run all the way to the clubhouse, she looked as fresh and cool as always.

How does she always manage to look so unruffled? Trixie thought as she involuntarily tucked in her own blouse and pulled up her socks. *I'm always such a frump!* She glanced at Jim, who must have been reading her thoughts, for he gave her a warm smile. Her confidence restored, she pounded an imaginary gavel on the ground to bring the meeting to order.

She and Honey brought everyone up to date on

the latest developments. It was Di who asked the
first question. "Where is Cliveden, Trixie? Is it anywhere near Williamsburg?"

"I'm not sure, but we can look it up," Trixie answered. "I brought a gasoline company road map,
just in case we needed it." She jumped up and, bringing the map from the basket of her bicycle, spread
it on the ground.

"There's Cliveden, and—yes, there's Williamsburg,
not very far away. Why, Di? Do you know anyone
there?" Honey asked hopefully.

"No," Di answered in her usual slow way, "but it
just happens that Daddy and Mummy are going to
Williamsburg tomorrow on a trip. There's some sort
of convention down there. They wanted me to go
along, as a matter of fact, because they thought it
would be good for me to see Washington and Williamsburg, but I got out of it. I'd much rather stay
here with you all."

Oh, no! Trixie thought. *If only I were in her shoes,
I'd go in a flash.* Aloud she said, "Oh, Di, couldn't you
change your mind? Maybe you could find out *something* about Rosewood Hall." As soon as she had said
it, she realized that she had sounded patronizing. She
hadn't meant to, although Di never had been as quick
as Honey to help solve a mystery. "Would you, Di?"
she asked as sincerely as she could.

"I'll do whatever I can, Trix, but I may have an
even better idea." The color rose in her cheeks, and
her lovely violet eyes were bright with excitement.

"Why don't I get Daddy and Mummy to take us all with them?"

"All the Bob-Whites?" Jim asked in amazement. "Something tells me your father wouldn't like the idea of that many on such a long trip."

"And besides," Brian continued, "we just got back from one vacation, and I'm not at all sure my parents would let us go off again. I know Dan won't be able to get any time off. What do you think, Trixie?"

Trixie had been unusually silent during the discussion. "I don't know," she answered, "but Mr. Lynch is a darling, and if Di thinks he might let us go, maybe he will, and if we act really enthusiastic and let our parents see what an educational advantage it would be—who knows? Maybe they'll say yes."

"You'll have to admit that they've been wonderful about letting us go off on trips to Arizona, Iowa, Cobbett's Island, and all," Mart said. "When could you ask your father, Di?" he added, and the excitement in his voice as he said it made Trixie realize that Mart was rapidly getting into the spirit of the adventure. She could count on him from now on.

"Well, he's home now, helping Mummy get ready. That's why I was late getting here. I was putting things in the back of the car," Di answered. "I could find out right away, I guess."

"Take my bike," Trixie offered, "and, for goodness' sake, don't worry if he says it's not a good idea. We'll understand and work out the problem some other way. We can come up with something else."

The Bob-Whites echoed Trixie's words as Di sped
off toward home, promising to phone Honey's house
as soon as she had talked with her parents. The meeting broke up almost immediately. Trixie and her
brothers walked back to Manor House with Honey
and Jim to await the news.

"Let's take a swim while we're waiting," Honey
suggested. "There's an extension phone in the bathhouse."

"Good idea, Honey," Brian said. "It'll make the
time go faster. I think all the Beldens have bathing
suits down there. We never bother to take them
home," he said with a laugh.

Honey, who was an expert swimmer, made a perfect swan dive into the shimmering water, and she
was quickly followed by Jim and Brian. Mart
emerged from the bathhouse last, wearing a faded
old suit that was much too big for him. Holding his
nose, he made a clownish jump into the water. Only
Trixie didn't go in. She hovered around the bathhouse, waiting for the phone to ring.

"Come on, Trix," Jim urged her. "You can't make
it ring any sooner by standing there. If you're not in
by the time I count ten, I'll come out and throw
you in!"

A half hour passed, and everyone was beginning
to get a little edgy, when the phone finally rang.
Trixie got to it first, but she held the receiver away
from her ear so the others could also hear what Di

had to say about her parents' reaction.

"It's okay!" Di cried. "Daddy and Mummy talked it over. That's what took so long, but I think we've finally got all the details worked out. Daddy wants this trip to be his treat, because my birthday is next week. We're going to take both cars so we won't be so crowded," she went on breathlessly. "Oh, Trixie, I've never been so excited in my life!"

"You think *you're* excited!" Trixie laughed. "You should see us. Mart just collapsed into a deck chair so hard he broke the legs, and the rest of us are absolutely bursting."

"Ask her when they plan to leave," Honey interrupted, "and don't forget, we still have to get permission to go along."

"Sometime tomorrow morning," Di said in answer to Trixie's question. "We'll be gone five or six days. Now, hurry and find out if you all can go. I'll simply die if you can't!"

"Now you sound like me, Di," Trixie chuckled. "I'm the one who's always 'dying'!" She promised to phone as soon as she had any news and told Di that Honey was already on her way up to her house to talk with Miss Trask. "Her parents are still in South America, you know," Trixie added.

Mr. and Mrs. Belden were unloading groceries and packages from the station wagon when Trixie and her brothers reached home. Trixie could scarcely contain herself until the purchases had been put away. Then, as her father sat down in the kitchen rocker and her mother started to put on her big white apron, preparatory to getting dinner, Trixie broached the question of the trip. By previous arrangement, Mart and Brian had gone out to feed the chickens. They knew that if any of them could get permission for the trip, it would be Trixie.

"Trixie, you look just like a kettle that's about to blow its lid off," her father said. "Out with it. What's simmering in that pretty little head of yours?"

"Oh, the most wonderful thing!" Trixie began. "Mr. and Mrs. Lynch have asked the Bob-Whites to go with them on a trip to Washington and then on to Williamsburg. Isn't that exciting?"

"It's very exciting, but I don't quite see—" Mrs. Belden began.

"It won't cost anything, because Mr. Lynch is giving the trip to Di for her birthday," Trixie said, anticipating one of the objections to the proposal.

"It isn't just the expense," her father said. "You and the boys have certain responsibilities around here, you know. It isn't fair for your mother to have to take over all the chores, is it?"

"I know it's not," Trixie conceded. "I guess I shouldn't have even asked, but it did sound like a good idea at the time."

"Now, Dad," Mrs. Belden said, "I can manage for another week. Bobby has finally learned the difference between a weed and a carrot top, and if you'll take over the chickens for those few days, I don't see why we wouldn't get along just fine."

"Oh, Moms, you're the *most!*" Trixie cried, giving her a hug. "You *will* see to the chickens, won't you, Dad, and maybe wash a dish or two?" she begged.

"Yes, princess. I guess you knew right from the first we'd say yes, didn't you?" her father chuckled.

"Well, I was *pretty* sure, and Mart and Brian and I will work extra hard when we get back, believe me!" Then she dashed out to the barn, slamming the porch door as she went, to give her brothers the good news.

Wonderful Washington • 6

NEEDLESS TO SAY, there was quite a scramble that evening as everyone got ready for the departure next day. Suitcases, only recently put away, were hauled out. Phones were ringing in all three houses to discuss what clothes should be taken, what time they were actually going to leave, and where they would be staying.

"The first night we'll be at a motel in Washington," Di told Trixie, "and it has a pool, so be sure you all bring bathing suits. When we get to Williamsburg, we'll stay at one of the cottages near the Inn. Daddy made reservations this morning."

"That sounds absolutely super!" Trixie exclaimed and then added, almost in a whisper, "And did you stop to think that, with two cars, we'll be able to explore to our hearts' content?"

"I know. Daddy said that while he and Mummy

are at the meetings, either Brian or Jim can drive us around. He says that since they took the driver's education course in school, they handle a car better than he does. Now I've got to run. See you tomorrow at nine."

It was a little after that hour when the Lynches drove down the Belden driveway. They had stopped first to pick up Honey and Jim, who were riding with Mrs. Lynch and Di in the convertible.

"Put your gear in the back and hop in," Mr. Lynch called out. "We'll change the seating arrangements as we go along, so everyone will have a chance to ride in Mother's new convertible. Isn't it a beauty? You don't mind starting out in the station wagon, do you, Trixie?"

"I'd start out in an oxcart," Trixie laughed, "just so we get there. I can't tell you how much we appreciate your taking us, Mr. Lynch." Then to herself she added, *If we do find the emeralds, he'll really know how important the trip is.*

Bags were quickly stowed, and, with much shouting of good-byes and waving of hands, they were away.

"What kind of convention is it you're going to, sir?" Brian asked as they drove out of town.

"Well, in the last couple of years I've become very interested in historic restorations," Mr. Lynch replied. "I've seen what the Rockefellers have done to restore Washington Irving's home and the old Van Cortlandt

Manor House right here in Westchester. So I joined
the County Historical Society. They're meeting with
several similar organizations to swap notes on what's
being done in various parts of the East. It should be
an interesting get-together."

"Our class visited Sunnyside last year," Trixie said.
"I could just imagine Washington Irving in his cozy
study, writing about Ichabod Crane and the headless
horseman. I think it's wonderful to save places like
that!"

"It surely is," Mr. Lynch agreed. "More and more
individuals and societies are coming to recognize the
need to keep historical landmarks from being torn
down in the name of what some people call progress."

The hours seemed to speed by as Mr. Lynch talked
and answered their questions, and it was soon lunchtime. By now they were on the turnpike from New
York to Washington and were making very good
time. They stopped at a restaurant along the way
and looked to see if, by any chance, Mrs. Lynch had
chosen the same place, but there was no sign of her
car in the parking lot.

"I told her not to try to follow us but just to plan
to meet us at the motel tonight," Mr. Lynch remarked
as they went in and were ushered to a large table
near a window.

Mart, realizing that he was Mr. Lynch's guest,
followed Trixie's lead and ordered a single hamburger and a glass of milk.

"Come now, you two," Mr. Lynch chuckled. "I

know you can eat more than that, Mart. You have something of a reputation to maintain. Order up, now, whatever you want, and hang the expense!"

Mr. Lynch is just as gay and jolly as he was before he got rich and moved into the big house with servants and everything, Trixie thought to herself. *I'll bet he likes getting away from all that formality for a few days.*

Mart waited until Trixie had changed her order to a double hamburger and a chocolate malt, then said, "I'll have the same—and an order of french fries, please."

"That's more like it," Mr. Lynch said with a smile. "Now, how about you, Brian?"

Brian, who was beginning to feel that hamburgers and hot dogs might be a little unsophisticated, ordered barbecued beef on a soft bun, with coleslaw.

"Why, Brian!" Trixie exclaimed. "Are you breaking the family tradition?"

"Not exactly. I just decided to be a little experimental on this trip," Brian answered suavely. "Who knows? I might discover a new taste sensation."

"If you find anything to top a hamburger, I'll eat my T-shirt with relish!" Mart said.

"If not with relish, maybe with catsup!" Trixie quipped.

While they were waiting for their food, Trixie looked out of the window to the service area of the restaurant. She was thinking what a dull job it must be to pump gas all day, when she noticed a rather

dilapidated horse van drive up. A boy carrying a
bucket jumped out of the right-hand side of the
truck. As he walked to the nearby garage to use the
water spigot, Trixie felt there was something familiar
about him. When he took off his cap to wipe his forehead, she knew immediately whom he reminded her
of. Neil! But how could that be? She started to say
something about it to the others but realized she
was the only one who had seen Neil that day at Miss
Julie's. Anyway, it was probably only a resemblance.
She reminded herself that Neil had said he was going
to stay in Croton all summer. Still, he *did* have that
craze for horses.

Trixie kept her eyes glued to the scene outside. The
boy took the bucket of water to the van and held it
while the horse inside drank his fill. The driver, a
thin-faced, rather sour-looking individual, leaned out
of the cab and motioned impatiently for him to
hurry. He was answered by a brusque shake of the
head as the boy patted the horse and let him finish
drinking. From the little pantomime, Trixie drew
some definite conclusions about the characters of
the two people involved. The whole thing gave her
an uneasy feeling; although she kept telling herself
that it was probably just a matter of strong physical
likeness, she still wasn't really sure the boy wasn't
Neil.

After they arrived at the motel late that afternoon
and were unpacking the station wagon, Mrs. Lynch

drove up with the others in her convertible.

"Well, you made good time, Mother," Mr. Lynch called out cheerily. "I didn't expect you for another hour, at least. You didn't break any speed laws, did you?"

"No, we didn't get a single ticket." She laughed. "The secret is that I let Jim take the wheel just south of New York, and you're right: He is a superb driver."

Mr. Lynch had reserved three rooms, one for himself and his wife, one for the boys, and the third for Trixie, Honey, and Di. Trixie gasped as she went into their room. She had never in her life seen such a luxurious motel. The furnishings were modern in style. Quilted turquoise bedspreads harmonized perfectly with the draperies and the thick rug. Attractive lamps and pictures and comfortable chairs gave the room a hospitable air. A sliding glass door opened onto a porch, from which they had easy access to the swimming pool.

"Why don't you all take a swim while Mother and I rest up a bit?" Mr. Lynch suggested. "Then we can go next door for dinner."

"That sounds great!" Mart cried. "Come on, gang. Last one in is a monkey!"

After a refreshing swim, they were relaxing by the side of the pool, and Trixie told them about the horse van at the restaurant.

"Oh, it couldn't have been Neil," Honey said. "How could he have gotten a job on a truck, living way back off the main road at Miss Julie's?"

"Well, you know our Trixie," Mart gibed. "She can't let a day go by without something mysterious happening. Incidentally, even if it *was*—I mean *were*—Neil what's-his-name, what's that got to do with the emeralds?"

"Oh, nothing, I suppose," Trixie said. "It's just one of those peculiar things that always bother me. They don't seem important at the time, and yet. . . ." Trixie's voice trailed off into silence.

"Well, that's all too vague to make me lose any sleep," Mart drawled, stretching out full length on the warm tiles.

"You don't have to lose any precious shut-eye," Brian told him in a slightly acid tone. "All we ask is that when you *are* awake, you make an attempt to keep your eyes open. You *might* pick up some information that would be helpful."

Mart took this dig in silence, but Di jumped to his defense.

"Oh, don't be hard on Mart. He may talk a lot, but you know he's come up with some good ideas in the past. Hasn't he, Trix?"

"He sure has," Trixie replied warmly, not wanting any quarrels to spoil the trip, "and I'm willing to bet he will again."

"Just so we'll all know what to look for," Di continued, "why don't you describe that old horse van in detail, Trixie?"

At first everyone laughed at Di's naïve suggestion. It seemed so unlikely that they'd ever see the truck again, but Trixie had second thoughts about it.

"Don't be so sure we won't bump into that pair again sometime," she said. "Stranger things have happened. Well, the van was dirty green and large enough for two horses, but there was only one in it today, a black one. At least, its head was black, and it had a white star on its face. The left taillight of the truck was broken. On the side of the van was the word 'Stable' in big white letters and another word had been painted out with black paint."

"Wow! How's that for a photographic memory?" Jim exclaimed. "How do you do it, Trix?"

"I'll let you in on the secret of my enormous success as a detective." She laughed. She felt the color rising in her cheeks at Jim's praise. "It's a kind of game. You see, I look at some new thing—a room, a person, or a scene like the van at the gas pump. Then after a few seconds I close my eyes and see how much I can remember of what I've seen. Then I check to see how accurate I've been. At first I'd leave out a lot of details, but the more I practiced, the better I got. Now a quick glance at something is all I need."

"That sounds like fun," Honey said enthusiastically. "Let's all start practicing. Why didn't you ever tell us about it before, Trixie?"

"Oh, I thought it was a little silly, I guess, but I've found I really *see* things now and don't just *look* at them," she answered.

Their discussion was broken up when they heard Mrs. Lynch call out that it was time to get dressed.

It was such a hot night that the girls decided to wear light blouses and skirts. Everyone took a long time over the delicious dinner. The restaurant was air-conditioned, and the soft music and excellent service made it a pleasant hour. As they came out, it was beginning to grow dark. Trixie, turning to Mr. Lynch, asked him if they could go for a walk along the Mall, which was quite near the motel.

"I've eaten so much that I need exercise," she laughed, "and besides, I'd love to see the Lincoln Memorial while I'm here in Washington."

"That will take us past the Washington Monument, too," Jim said after Mr. Lynch had urged them to look around the neighborhood.

Although the Bob-Whites had seen many pictures of the capital city, none of them had actually been there, so the experience was a new one for them all. It was a beautiful evening, with a three-quarter moon shining in a cloudless sky and a soft breeze from the Potomac River beginning to cool the air. No one said anything as they approached the awesome figure of Lincoln. They were silent, too, as they read the inscription on the wall behind the great stone chair: "In this temple as in the hearts of the people for whom he saved the Union the memory of Abraham Lincoln is inscribed forever."

Walking out between the tall columns that supported the roof, Trixie said, "Just think, the Civil War hadn't even begun when Ruth and John went to Virginia."

"And since then we've been involved in one war after another," Brian added. "I wonder where it will end."

"Well, I hope it ends in peace for the whole world!" Mart said with unusual seriousness. Then, looking toward the White House, which they were approaching, he continued, "I'd sure hate to be President of the United States. It must be the hardest job in the world."

"I don't think you have to worry about *that*," Trixie said, giving her brother a good-natured pat on the shoulder. "At least not for quite a while." The walk back to the motel ended on a lighter note.

They spent the next day sight-seeing. The boys wanted especially to see the airplanes at the Smithsonian Institution, so in the morning they took leave of the girls, who went to the National Gallery of Art. The Bob-Whites had decided the evening before, while talking with Mr. Lynch, that it would be a mistake to try to visit too many places in the one day they had in the city. Everyone agreed, however, that the newly decorated White House was a must, so they arranged to meet after lunch and all go there together.

Trixie had somehow imagined they would be able to stroll through the White House in much the same way that her class had done at Washington Irving's restored home, but she found this tour quite different. Later, when told that over half a million people had already visited the White House that year, Trixie understood why there was little time to linger in any one room. In the Lincoln bedroom, however, she could not resist hanging back for a longer look. Jim, who had stayed in the forefront of the group to catch every word their guide had to say, came back to where she was solemnly gazing at an intricately carved rosewood table that Mrs. Lincoln had bought.

"Why so glum, Trixie?" he asked. "Are you getting tired?"

"Oh, no! I'm fine!" she answered, her face brightening. "I was only thinking about Rosewood Hall. Do you suppose we'll find it's one of the lucky places that someone has loved enough to preserve like this?"

"I hope so, but we may not even find it, you know," Jim replied. "As Mr. Lynch said, many beautiful old homes were either burned during the war or fell into ruins afterward."

"I'll simply *die* if we don't find *something* left at Rosewood," Trixie said.

For answer, Jim patted her shoulder, and they hurried on to join the others in the next room.

"Get Out of Here!" • 7

WILLIAMSBURG is only a hundred and fifty miles from Washington, so by noon the next day everyone was settled into a comfortable Colonial cottage near the Inn. Trixie, of course, was eager to drive out to Cliveden without delay, but she cheerfully fell in with the plan of the others to walk around the old streets of the town and become familiar with the layout before going through any of the buildings. They had great fun outside the Public Gaol, taking turns being locked in the pillory and the stocks. Honey had brought her camera and took pictures of them and the "gaoler," a guide dressed in Colonial garb. The whole village occupied an area only a mile and a half wide, so even though they walked slowly and absorbed all the sights, they were through with their tour early in the afternoon.

"Don't you think we might drive out to Cliveden

this afternoon and just have a look at the place?"
Trixie asked. "We can easily get back in time for
dinner."

"Why not?" Di asked eagerly. "Daddy and
Mummy will be at a tea until six, so we'll have plenty
of time."

They stopped at the large brick restoration that,
from 1699 to 1780, had served as the capitol of the
Virginia colony and asked one of the guides the way
to Cliveden.

"It's not far out on the dirt road south of here," he
told them. "But you'll have to watch out, or you'll
drive right through without knowing it. I don't reckon
there's more than a couple of hundred people in the
whole township, and they're pretty well scattered."

"That doesn't sound too promising, does it?" Honey
asked as they walked back to their cottage to pick up
the station wagon and leave a note for Mr. and Mrs.
Lynch.

"But there's bound to be a post office in the town,"
Trixie answered. "Maybe someone there will know
where Rosewood Hall is." She tried to keep the note
of discouragement out of her voice as she said this.

The guide had been right. Cliveden was not much
bigger than the dot on the map in the geography
book. If Trixie hadn't happened to notice a rusty
sign, INCORPORATED VILLAGE OF CLIVEDEN, SPEED
LIMIT 15 MILES AN HOUR, they might well have driven
right through.

"Wow! Fifteen miles an hour!" Jim exclaimed,

slowing the car to a crawl. "I bet that sign has been there since the first horseless carriage came into town."

"Watch out for the livestock!" Brian cautioned as a rawboned old cow meandered onto the road.

"Looks more like dead stock to me," Mart said with a shiver. "What a creepy town!"

There were a few houses and one general store, a boarded-up church, and a one-pump gas station. As they passed the store, Trixie caught sight of a small sign in the window: UNITED STATES POST OFFICE.

"Gleeps!" she cried. "Back up, Jim, or turn around or something. We're on the right track at last."

"Hey, watch out, Trix!" Brian yelled as Trixie opened the door and jumped out almost before the car had come to a halt. "Do you want to lose a leg?"

His warning was disregarded as his sister raced up the rickety steps into the store.

"Let's stay in the car," Honey suggested. "If there *is* a Rosewood Hall, she should be the first one to hear about it, and if there *isn't,* our being in there with her won't help matters a bit."

"You're right, Honey," Jim said. "I hope she'll get some encouragement. She's so sure she's on the trail of something big; I'd hate to see her bubble burst now."

The store was empty when Trixie entered, but the squeak of the hinge apparently had been heard by someone in the rear, because it wasn't many seconds before there was the sound of scuffing feet. A curtain hanging in a doorway at the back was pushed aside, and a wrinkled-faced old woman came out. Although the day was hot, she clutched a faded blue shawl around her thin shoulders.

"Excuse me," Trixie began, her voice unnaturally high with excitement. "Do you happen to know where Rosewood Hall is?"

"Rosewood Hall?" The old lady cackled. "I reckon I *do* know where it is. My folks used to live there before—" She gave Trixie a long, cold look, the smile disappearing from her face. "What do you-all want to know about Rosewood Hall for?" she drawled. "You aren't from around here, are you?"

"No, we're just passing through," Trixie answered as nonchalantly as she could. "Relatives of a friend of mine used to live there, and I was curious to see it, that's all."

She smiled sweetly and turned as though to leave, hoping to reassure the old lady that she didn't have any ulterior motive in asking about Rosewood.

"Not so fast, honey," the woman said, coming out from behind the nearly empty showcase, the wry smile reappearing. "I thought you might be another of those rich folks from up north."

"Well, I'm from up north," Trixie said in her most ingratiating manner, "but I'm certainly far from being rich!"

"They come down here and buy up these old places, and us folks who've lived in 'em for years have to get out," the old lady said in a whining voice. "Then they don't even have the grace to come in here to buy a stamp."

"Is that what happened to you?" Trixie asked.

"Well, not exactly," was the evasive reply. "Part of Rosewood burned down during the Civil War, and the wing that was left, where we lived, just finally fell down around our ears when I was a girl. Rotten clean through, it was. There's only the front left standing today."

Trixie's heart was pounding as she said, "Well, I'd like to take a look at it, as long as I've come this far."

"It'll just be a waste of time, honey. If you want to see a really nice place, go to the house next to it, Green Trees. That's one the Northerners haven't got their hands on yet."

"And who lives there?" Trixie asked, wanting to get as much information as possible from what might turn out to be her only source.

"Edgar Carver, and he's the last of his line," the old woman said sadly. "I'm told his ancestors built the house over a hundred and fifty years ago, and there's been a Carver in it ever since. It's down the road a mile. You can't miss it."

"Oh, thank you, Miss—"

"James, honey, Lizzie James, and if you see Edgar, tell him I said hello." And with that she shuffled off behind the curtain. So far as she was concerned, the interview was over.

As Trixie came out of the store, the Bob-Whites

couldn't tell from her looks what her luck had been. She walked slowly toward them, a trace of a frown on her forehead, but she didn't keep them in suspense long.

"Well, it's both good and bad news," she said as she settled into her seat with a sigh. "I found out where Rosewood Hall is, all right, but—" she paused, and tears welled up in her eyes—"it's nothing but a ruin!"

"Oh, Trixie," Honey cried sympathetically, putting her arm around her friend. "I had *so* hoped—"

"Let's drive on down the road, anyway," Trixie said, dabbing her eyes and forcing a smile. "We might as well know the worst."

They had not gone far before they noticed what appeared to be a newly installed post-and-rail fence running along the road. The grass in the field behind it had been recently cut. Two horses, their noses poking through the fence, were browsing on the taller grass outside.

"There's a living example of the old saying about the grass on the other side of the fence," laughed Brian. "I wonder who owns this farm. Looks prosperous, doesn't it?"

A little farther on they came to a break in the fence; instead of a gate, there was a heavy chain across the opening.

Jim stopped the car so they could look down the driveway beyond. Suddenly Trixie, who had got out of the car with the others, called out, "Way back there in that clump of trees! Don't you see something white?"

"You're right, Trix," Jim said, craning his neck to get a better view. "I'll bet it's Rosewood Hall."

"Well, if it's in ruins, certainly no one is living there now," Trixie said. "If we don't bother the horses, I don't think anyone would mind if we walked in and looked at it, do you?" She turned to the other Bob-Whites for reassurance.

"Of course not. Come on," Mart urged. "There's not apt to be anyone around. Except for the horses, this place looks absolutely deserted." He jumped over the chain and headed for the ruins.

The others quickly followed. What had once been a sweeping driveway was now little more than a path, barely wide enough for a car. A tangle of rhododendron and laurel bushes grew on either side of the winding road, with magnolia trees and pines behind them. The air was redolent with a scent which none of them recognized.

"It must be jasmine," Honey conjectured. "Books about the South always talk about the smell of jasmine and honeysuckle."

Their conversation was interrupted as they rounded a wide curve and suddenly came upon a sight that held them all breathless. There, in the wilderness of green, was what looked to be the remains of a Greek temple. Five white Doric columns rose from a stone veranda, their stark lines softened now by wisteria which had grown around them for years. Two others had fallen and lay cracked and broken on the ground.

"What a beautiful place this must have been," Trixie sighed as she picked her way through the vines and climbed the wide steps. "Can't you just imagine girls in crinolines and elegant young men sitting here?"

"You're *so* romantic!" Mart teased. "You sound like Scarlett in *Gone With the Wind,* but I'll admit it's beautiful."

"Let's go around back and see if any of the foundations of the house are left," Jim suggested. "We may get a better idea of what the place looked like." He started to make his way through the underbrush behind the columns.

Jim was right. Not only were the outside foundations clearly visible, but the supporting posts in what had been the cellar also gave an indication of the way the rooms had been laid out.

A sudden yell from Trixie brought them all over to where she stood.

"Look! Someone has started clearing around here!" she cried. "See where all those vines have been cut back? And some of these stones have been moved recently; you can see fresh dirt on top of them."

The Bob-Whites were so busy examining Trixie's find that they failed to hear approaching footsteps until a rough voice snarled, "Hey, you! Get out of here, or I'll have the law on you!"

They wheeled around to see a man on horseback brandishing a heavy riding crop. Trixie couldn't be

sure whether his face was so red because of sunburn, natural coloration, or anger, but she strongly
suspected the last. His coarse black hair, growing
low on his forehead, looked as if it had never known a
comb, and it was hard to imagine that the small eyes,
glaring from under heavy brows, had ever smiled.
Jim took a step forward, a move which only served
to make the man raise the whip again, but Jim was
undaunted.

"We beg your pardon, sir. We certainly meant no
harm. My friends and I were curious about the house
that used to stand here."

"Curiosity killed the cat, and it's just as likely to get
you into trouble, too," the man snapped. "This is a
horse farm, not a tourist joint, and I don't want
nobody prying around here. Do you understand?"

Trixie, who had come up beside Jim, said, "We
certainly do understand. You've made it very clear,
and we'll be delighted to leave, but just so we won't
make the mistake of trespassing again, you'd better
show us where your property ends."

The man looked at her suspiciously, as if to make
sure, before answering, that she wasn't making fun
of him. Although Trixie's face was flaming, it was
dead serious, and she didn't flinch under his scrutiny.

"You won't have no trouble if you keep outside the
fence," he replied. "The whole farm is closed in, all
sixty acres of it. Cost me a pretty penny, it did, too, to
have it surveyed and fenced, but I don't want no
mistake about what's mine. Now, get going. There's

the path to the main road, right over there."

He pointed over his shoulder to the lane, a continuation of the one the Bob-Whites had taken when they came in. Yanking the reins, he wheeled the beautiful roan he was riding and watched until they were on the path and walking toward the entrance. Then, striking the horse sharply, he galloped off in the opposite direction.

"Whew! That's Southern hospitality for you!" Mart exclaimed. "This trip has been about as useful as a refrigerator at the North Pole."

Trixie, her hands clenched and her head down, kicked the dirt angrily as she walked along. She didn't join the others as they discussed the unpleasant incident. She was torn between a feeling of great sadness at the sight of the ruins of Rosewood and fury at the incivility of the owner. She couldn't bear to admit that this might be the one and only chance they would have to visit Rosewood Hall. As she thought about it, she suddenly realized they wouldn't even be able to look for the graveyard Ruth and Helen had visited those long years ago. In her mind's eye, she could still see the faded entry in John Sunderland's diary. She felt utterly miserable.

"Cheer up, Trixie," Di urged her. "I know how you feel, but don't let it spoil our holiday."

Trixie, remembering that this trip was Di's birthday present and that she shouldn't put her own feelings first, made an effort to appear cheerful.

"You're right, Di," she said, forcing a smile. "Let's

forget that old grouch and take a look at Green Trees."

"And this time I suggest that we don't even get out of the car," Brian said with a shake of his head. "We're apparently in enemy territory."

A short distance down the road, they came to the end of the fenced-in land, and not far beyond was Green Trees, set far back from the road among well-tended lawns and shrubbery. Jim pulled the car to the side of the road and turned off the motor.

"Look!" Trixie cried. "It's just what Rosewood Hall must have been like. Aren't those the same kind of columns?"

"They certainly are!" Honey agreed. "What a gorgeous house!"

"Wouldn't you love to go through it?" Di said. "But I wouldn't even dare to ask, after the reception we just got. Would you, Trixie?"

"No, but we won't *have* to ask, Di," Trixie said softly.

"What do you mean?" Mart asked incredulously.

Trixie had been sitting next to the window in the front seat and had spotted a small sign which the others hadn't noticed. Everyone craned their necks to see it after Trixie had pointed it out.

GREEN TREES, it read. OPEN TO THE PUBLIC THURSDAYS 1 TO 3. ADMISSION $1.

"And today's Wednesday." Jim broke the silence. "We can drive out again tomorrow afternoon. You know, we're in luck!"

"Yes, I guess we are," Trixie answered a little dubiously. She didn't know then just *how* lucky their forthcoming tour of Green Trees would be.

They were awakened the next morning by the firing of the cannon salute on the Market Square Green. At breakfast, Mr. Lynch asked the Bob-Whites about their expedition into the country the day before. He and Mrs. Lynch had gone to an official dinner the previous night, so this was the first opportunity he had had to hear about their activities.

"Oh, we saw the most beautiful house," Trixie began. "It's only a few miles from here, and it's open to the public. They call it Green Trees."

"It's just what I always imagined a Southern mansion would look like," Honey said, "all white and shining and gracious looking."

"I've heard of Green Trees," Mr. Lynch said. "I believe the local historical society has had a lot to do with restoring it."

"It certainly looks as though someone has taken wonderful care of the place," Brian commented. "It was in apple-pie order—lawns, hedges, everything. Of course, we didn't see the inside."

"No, but today is visiting day," Di told her father, "so we're going back this afternoon. I wish you could go with us, Daddy; you and Mummy would love it!"

"I wish I could, too, Diana, but they've set up a very tight schedule for us here. I'll try to see it before we leave for home. I promise you."

Since they couldn't tour Green Trees until one o'clock, the Bob-Whites had plenty of time after breakfast to go through the many fascinating buildings in Williamsburg. As they stepped into the wigmaker's shop, it was as if they had suddenly been transported back to Colonial days. The man at the workbench was dressed in authentic eighteenth century clothes—a full-sleeved white shirt, knee pants, and heavy white stockings. On his shoes were buckles of silver. They watched as he repaired a black wig set on a wooden wig stand before him.

"Did the children wear wigs in those days, too?" Mart asked.

The wigmaker looked over the top of his glasses at Mart.

"No, not the little ones." He smiled. "Here, take this and try it on." He handed Mart a wig he had taken from the display in the window of the shop. It was dark brown, with waves on the side and a little red bow tied to the short pigtail in the back. It so altered Mart's appearance that everyone burst out laughing.

"Whoever thought I'd be caught in a peruke!" Mart said as he stuck his fingers inside his shirtfront and assumed an exaggerated pose.

"A *what?*" Di asked, wide-eyed.

"The young gentleman is quite right," the wigmaker said. "Wigs were sometimes called perukes or periwigs. And did you know that wigmakers also used to serve as barbers and surgeons?"

"Well, they must have cut quite a figure," Mart quipped. "Who was the first one to dream up the idea of a wig, anyway?"

"That's something no one will ever know," the man replied. "Egyptian mummies have been found wearing them, and there is evidence that wigs were worn by both the Greeks and the Romans. So, you see, they go way back to antiquity."

"Why do you suppose people started wearing them?" Di asked. "I'd rather dress my own hair up fancy than wear one of *those* things." She tossed her lovely hair over her shoulders as she spoke.

"Not everyone is blessed with beautiful hair like yours," the wigmaker said with a smile, "so false hair sometimes helped to correct nature's defects. Wigs are still used in the English courts, and, of course, the theater couldn't get along without them."

"I never realized there was so much to learn about wigs," Honey said as they thanked the man and started to leave. "Come to think of it, now that they're back in style, how do you think I'd look as a redhead?"

"Perfectly ghastly!" Brian cried. "You stay just the way you are, Honey Wheeler, or you'll be expelled from the Bob-Whites!"

From the wigmaker's shop, they went to the ten other shops Williamsburg boasted, where they saw craftsmen, using authentic antique equipment, weaving cloth, working in silver, or fashioning iron pieces at the old forge. By the time they had seen the Governor's Palace and the Raleigh Tavern and a few other attractions, it was time for lunch.

"Let's eat at Chowning's. It's just down the street a way," Di suggested. "Daddy said they serve lunch outdoors, under an arbor."

"Do we have time?" Trixie asked, looking anxiously at her wristwatch. "I'm dying to get back to Green Trees in time for the tour."

"There's plenty of time, Trix," Mart answered. "It's eleven thirty, and you know it only takes a few minutes to drive out there. Besides, I wouldn't skip lunch for anything."

"Not even for the emeralds?" Honey asked.

"Well, now you really put me on the spot." Mart laughed. "I guess I could skip one meal if I had to, but that doesn't mean I'd enjoy it."

"I don't think you'll have to be put to the test," Trixie said disconsolately. "It looks as though we'd better forget the emeralds. There always has to be a first time for everything, you know, and this will go down as the Bob-Whites' first failure."

"I refuse to believe it," Honey said with a toss of her head.

"What makes you so sure?" Brian asked. "Give me one good reason for optimism, and I'll treat you to a banana split—triple-scoop king-sized."

"Oh, nothing tangible, really. It's just a hunch," Honey replied as they approached the restaurant. "But it's a strong one, believe me."

"Welcome to Green Trees!" • 8

THERE WAS only one other car in the driveway at Green Trees when the Bob-Whites arrived.

"I'm glad there isn't a big crowd," Trixie commented as they approached the house. "You can see a lot more when there aren't too many people."

Jim had no sooner rapped on the door with the big brass knocker than it was opened wide, and the Bob-Whites had their first glimpse inside. It was a glimpse that gave them all something of a shock, for the man who admitted them was in a wheelchair. His legs were covered by a woolen afghan, so that only the tips of his slipper-shod feet were visible.

"Welcome to Green Trees. I am your host, Edgar Carver," he said, lifting his hands in a wide gesture of hospitality. "How nice to see so many young people! Would you like to sign the register there on the table? Then we will join the couple in the next room for the tour." Trixie thought she had never heard a more delightful voice.

While Jim and the others were signing, she had a chance to observe their host more closely.

"We're so glad to be here, Mr. Carver," she said warmly. "It's a real experience for us to see a house like this."

It was difficult for her to guess his age and equally difficult to believe him a cripple, for his shoulders were broad and strong-looking. His thick hair was quite gray, but there were remarkably few signs of aging in his handsome face. His deep blue eyes were clear and shining.

"We drove by yesterday, after stopping to look at Rosewood Hall," Trixie said, "and, I must say, our reception here is a lot more cordial than the one we got from your neighbor!"

At the words "Rosewood Hall," Mr. Carver leaned forward, his face sober.

"How did you know about Rosewood Hall?" he asked gently. "From your accent, I'm sure you're not from Virginia."

"No, we live a few miles outside New York City," Trixie answered, "but I found a letter, and then I found Miss Sunderland and—well, it's a long story."

"But a story which I should like to hear more about," Edgar Carver replied earnestly. "I must take these people on the tour now, but will you stay on afterward and tell me of your discovery? You see, my mother was born in Rosewood Hall, and *her* mother was a Sunderland."

"Of course I will," Trixie replied as Mr. Carver started toward the door. "I'll tell you everything that's happened."

Although his wheelchair was an old-fashioned one with a high wicker back and large wheels, the man managed it skillfully.

He must have been crippled for a long time, Trixie thought to herself as she watched him deftly turn it around and guide it through the door into the next room.

The waiting couple proved to be a friendly middle-aged man and his wife, a Mr. and Mrs. Sellers, who were visiting various out-of-the-way places on their leisurely trip to Florida, where they planned to spend the winter. Mr. Sellers had been an architect before retiring and was interested in old and historic houses. He was likable, but Trixie wished he wouldn't ask quite so many questions! She was dying to talk further with Edgar Carver. However, she didn't let her impatience keep her from noting every detail of the beautiful house.

As they went into yet another room, Mr. Carver explained that not all of Green Trees had been restored. This music room, for instance, was to be the next project of the historical society, but even in its present state of disrepair, it was charming. The paneled walls had been painted a soft green. An old spinet stood against one wall, and a harp with most of its strings broken was nearby. The rich gold-colored brocades at the windows and on the few pieces of furniture were faded and split, and the delicate crystal chandelier was dull with dust.

"Does Green Trees have a ghost?" Mrs. Sellers asked as they were leaving the music room. "So many of the old houses we've visited claim to have a family spook."

Edgar Carver laughed. "I know that ghosts, real or imaginary, are very fashionable in many of our old houses," he answered. "Perhaps that's why I've always been a bit hesitant about mentioning *our* ghost."

"Oh, then there is one here?" Honey cried. "Please tell us about it, Mr. Carver."

"I'm afraid it isn't a very romantic ghost," he began. "Nothing like the lovelorn maidens whose spirits swish in and out of drawing rooms, blowing out candles and striking chords on pianos and such. No, ours is a very ordinary ghost. He is said to have been one of the masons who worked on this house. Unfortunately, the poor fellow was killed when a large stone fell on him. It's believed that his spirit sometimes returns to Green Trees, and some say you can hear the tapping of his trowel on the stones."

"Have *you* ever heard him?" Di asked, wide-eyed.

"No," Mr. Carver said slowly. "I think I'm probably much too incredulous about such things to hear any but the most ordinary noises."

The last room they were shown had originally been a solarium, but now it was obviously being used as a

studio. There were still a few plants growing in large
tubs—a lemon tree, some gardenias, ferns, and an
avocado, which gave the room a tropical atmosphere.
A large easel with an unfinished painting on it occupied one corner, where the north light was brightest,
and near it stood a table on casters, covered with
tubes of paint, brushes, and bottles.

"This is where I spend a great deal of my time,"
Mr. Carver said as the party was invited in. "Without my painting, time would hang very heavy on my
hands, living out here in the country as I do."

There was not now, nor had there been at any
time during the tour, the slightest hint of self-pity in
Edgar Carver's voice. Trixie wondered if he lived
here all alone. In fact, there were a great many
things about him she wanted to know.

One wall of the solarium was filled with paintings,
and they immediately caught the eye of Mr. Sellers,
who went over and examined them with interest.

"Look here, Edith," he said, drawing his wife's
attention to one particular picture. It was a small
still life, a vase of white peonies against a reddish
background, beautifully painted in an impressionistic
style.

"How exquisite!" she exclaimed. "I would love to
have that."

Turning to Mr. Carver, she explained, "You see,
my husband and I are collectors in a modest way,
and we enjoy buying paintings that we discover
ourselves, but I don't suppose you want to part with

any of your own, do you?"

"Most artists, I believe, like to sell their work," Mr. Carver replied with a smile, "if not for fame, then for fortune. As a matter of fact," he continued, looking down at his hands folded in his lap, "I rather depend on the sale of my work. The historical society has been most generous in restoring Green Trees, but I cannot accept their help for my personal needs."

Trixie, sensing how embarrassing this discussion must be for him, interrupted to say she wanted to have another look at the old harp, and, with a sign to the other Bob-Whites to come with her, she left Mr. and Mrs. Sellers to consummate the sale of the picture.

"I don't see how anyone ever learns to play one of these things," Mart said as he went over to the harp and twanged one or two of the remaining strings.

"Oh, I'd love to have one," Di sighed. "They're *so* romantic!"

"Aren't they, though!" Mart mimicked her, plunking away at the ancient instrument, tossing his head and rolling his eyes, like an inspired musician. "Brian, why don't you-all ask Miss Lynch for the next waltz? I'm sure she'd be ever so enchanted."

Everyone was so amused at Mart's antics that they failed to notice that Trixie had left the group and had gone over to the window on the far side of the room. Then suddenly they saw her, half hidden behind the drapery, wildly waving her hands for them to be silent. She sidled along the wall toward the others, as though she wanted to avoid being seen from outside, and then motioned them into the hall.

Once out of the music room, Honey whispered, "What in the world did you see, Trix?"

"It was *Neill*" Trixie gasped. "This time I'm absolutely sure! He was hiding in the shrubbery outside that window, spying on Mr. Carver in the solarium!"

"Quiet!" Brian warned. "Here comes Mr. Carver with the Sellerses."

"Act as if nothing has happened," Trixie whispered, "until we know what's going on."

The Sellerses were ready to depart, and it took but a few minutes for good-byes to be said. After the great door closed behind them, Mr. Carver turned to Trixie. "Now, young lady," he said, almost boyishly enthusiastic, "won't you and your friends join me in my study? I must hear about your interest in Rosewood Hall." Leading them past the solarium, he went into a smaller, comfortably furnished room that had not been a part of the tour.

"This is my real hideaway." He smiled, motioning them to be seated. Then, again addressing Trixie, he said, "Tell me, do your friends know about Rosewood Hall, too?"

"Oh, yes," she replied eagerly. "As a matter of fact, we work together. We call ourselves the Bob-Whites."

"What do you mean by 'work together'?" Edgar

Carver asked a bit apprehensively.

"That *does* make it sound as though we were some kind of gang, doesn't it, sir?" Jim answered with a smile. "But I assure you we're not."

"We call our club the Bob-Whites, and it's Trixie here who gets us involved in all sorts of situations," Honey said. "She seems to attract mysteries like a magnet attracts nails."

"A mystery, eh?" Mr. Carver said. "Well, let's not waste any more time. Trixie, suppose you start from the beginning and tell me about the letter you mentioned earlier."

With a glance at the others, as though for reassurance, Trixie took from her handbag the ancient missive she had found in the attic and handed it to Edgar Carver.

When he had finished reading it, he looked up at Trixie, perplexity shadowing his face. She didn't wait for him to put his question into words but began to tell him the story of her discovery of the letter.

"You see, Moms and I were cleaning our attic a few days before we came down here. We live in a house that must be even older than this one, and while I was trying to open a sticky drawer, I lost my balance and fell back against the wall."

"She broke a couple of boards to smithereens!" Mart said. "But trust our Trixie to turn an accident into a mystery!"

"Well, it *did* turn out that way," Trixie continued with a smile. "Back of the broken board was a little

room that no one knew anything about, and in there
I found some old clothes from Civil War days and a
canteen and stuff. When I was taking them out, this
letter dropped out of one of the pockets."

"How strange that it should literally have come to
light after all these years," Mr. Carver mused. "But
how did you track down Julie Sunderland?" he asked.

"Luck was with us," Trixie continued. "Honey and
I looked up the last name in the phone book and
found there was one Sunderland listed in Croton,
and, when we investigated, we found it was Miss
Julie."

"She's terribly old, but a perfect darling," Honey
said. "She didn't remember too much that was helpful, but she did lend us some diaries her father had
kept, and they gave us the clue that Rosewood Hall
was in Cliveden."

"We might not have been able to go any further,"
Trixie said, "except that Di's father just happened to
be coming to Williamsburg for a convention, and Di
sort of—"

"Sort of sold him on the idea of taking all the Bob-
Whites with him?" Mr. Carver asked with a smile.

"You've penetrated our plot," Mart said. "Yes,
that's what happened, and the fact that Di's birthday
was coming up helped, too. Mr. and Mrs. Lynch gave
her the trip for a present."

Mr. Carver was silent for some time, apparently
lost in thought. Then, with a slight shake of his
head, he said, "Well, what you have told me begins

to answer some of the questions I have long asked myself. Ever since I was a little boy I've heard rumors about a charmed necklace or, you might say, a cursed necklace." He glanced down at his paralyzed legs.

"Not that I've taken too much stock in the story, mind you, but in my condition it does make one think, doesn't it?"

He paused, then went on, speaking slowly and thoughtfully.

"My great-grandfather, Jonathan Carver," he said, "built Green Trees, and his dearest friend, Charles Fields, built Rosewood Hall. They were known as the Twin Houses until the Civil War, when most of Rosewood was burned."

"Then there haven't been any Fieldses living there for many years, have there?" Trixie asked.

"No. Lee Fields, who brought Ruth Sunderland there as a bride, was killed in the war, and Ruth—" he sighed—"died soon after the birth of their only child, a daughter. . . ."

Mr. Carver's voice trailed off, and, seemingly unaware of the Bob-Whites, he gazed abstractedly out of the window. Trixie glanced around the little circle. Even the irrepressible Mart, for once in his life, was silent. Then, taking a long breath, Trixie said softly, "Ruth's baby, Mr. Carver—whatever became of her?"

A gentle smile touched his face. "Ruth's baby was my mother, Trixie."

"Then you and Miss Julie are related," Trixie said, her eyes shining.

"Yes, she would be my mother's cousin," Mr. Carver replied slowly.

"And what happened to Rosewood?" Trixie asked gently.

"It was willed to my father, and after the war, the one wing that remained standing was occupied by a succession of poor folks, who couldn't afford anything better."

"I think I met one of them yesterday," Trixie said, "a Miss Lizzie James, and she said if we saw you, to say hello for her."

"Poor old Lizzie." Mr. Carver sighed. "Life hasn't been too kind to her. I try to give her what business I can, but her stock is limited, to say the least, and I don't get to the store very often."

Trixie had been waiting to ask about the red-faced man they had encountered the day before at Rosewood Hall. At her question, a scowl came over Mr. Carver's face, and he pounded the arm of his chair with his fist as he said angrily, "That character! I was forced to sell Rosewood Hall about two years ago, because I could no longer pay the taxes. It's been years since I've even been able to keep up the grounds. The place was on the market for months, but no one was interested until this man Jenkins came along. He wanted to buy it because the stables and some of the outbuildings were still standing, and he had some notion of starting a horse farm. I regret the day I ever met the man. From all accounts, he's no good at all!"

"Does he run the place all by himself?" Trixie asked, hoping to find out if Neil was working there.

"He's the boss," Mr. Carver said, "but I've seen other men, or boys, exercising the horses. I really don't know what the setup is. The less I see of Jenkins the better."

Silence fell on the little group, and Trixie, looking at her watch, noted that it was twenty minutes past three.

"Time we should be leaving," she commented. "I can't tell you how disappointed I am that we can't go on with the search for the necklace, Mr. Carver, but with old Jenkins owning Rosewood, it looks pretty hopeless, doesn't it?"

"No," Mr. Carver replied thoughtfully, "not necessarily, *not necessarily.*"

"Why, we can't even try to find the directions Ruth mentioned," Trixie pointed out.

"I think perhaps you can," Mr. Carver said, a smile beginning to light up his face. "You see, when I divided the two properties and sold Rosewood, I made sure the old family burying ground was on *my* side of the line!"

At the Cemetery • 9

OH, NO!" Trixie, jumping to her feet, impulsively took one of Mr. Carver's hands in hers. "Then you don't mind? We can go on with the hunt?"

"Of course you may, my dear," he answered, "although I confess I feel somewhat the same way Miss Julie did. All this happened such a long time ago. But I can see you're not one to be easily discouraged."

"I wouldn't say Trixie is *never* discouraged," Mart broke in, "but she bounces back like a new tennis ball. When do you think we might get started, sir?"

"You seem to have considerable bounce, too," Mr. Carver said, sensing Mart's enthusiasm. "I want you Bob-Whites to feel free to come to Green Trees whenever you like. I'll help you all I can, but you realize that my contribution must, of necessity, be somewhat limited. It's a bit difficult for me to get around anywhere, except here in the house."

"Don't you worry about that, Mr. Carver," Trixie assured him. "Just tell us where the cemetery is, and we'll come back tomorrow and see if we can find any clues."

Edgar Carver wheeled himself over to a French door that looked out over a wide expanse of lawn to a clump of trees in the distance.

"Beyond those cryptomeria trees, close to the fence between Green Trees and Rosewood Hall, you'll find it," he said, pointing out the stately, tall evergreens.

"What kind of trees?" Mart asked. "I don't think I've ever heard that name before."

"Cryptomeria," Mr. Carver repeated. "I've often wondered if they were called that because they are frequently planted in cemeteries, where there are crypts."

"It could be," Mart said with interest. "I'll look it up when I get home."

"Now, when you get here tomorrow, I shall have the key to the vault for you," Mr. Carver continued. "The door hasn't been opened since my father's funeral, many, many years ago, so it may give you some trouble."

"We'll stop in town and get a can of penetrating oil," Brian said. "That's sure to work."

"What in the world is penetrating oil?" Honey asked.

"It's a special kind of oil for loosening up metal parts that have stuck or rusted," Brian explained. "I couldn't get along without it, working on parts for my old car."

"How is it different from just plain old oil?" Di asked.

"I know the answer to that one," Mart broke in eagerly. "Penetrating oil has a different molecular structure, so it can get into microscopic openings in the metal, where ordinary oil won't go."

"I can see Brian is the practical member of your team, and it looks as though Mart were the scientist." Mr. Carver laughed. "Am I right?"

"Well, actually, Brian is going to be a doctor," Honey said proudly, "but when he isn't reading medical books, he's usually working on his old jalopy. He can do anything with a motor."

"And there's no telling what Mart will turn out to be," Brian said, giving his brother a poke in the ribs. "He *says* he wants to be a farmer, but the way he throws big words around, we're sure he'll be a famous author. Then the next minute we're convinced his future lies with the circus. He's a real clown!"

"And *my* guess is that he'll end up running a restaurant." Trixie giggled. "He loves food better than anything else in the world!"

Edgar Carver saw the little group to the door and suggested that when they returned the next day, they come directly around to his study. "I'll be there or in my studio," he added, "and it will save me going all the way to the front of the house if you use the side door."

It was only after the Bob-Whites were in the station wagon and had started back to Williamsburg that Trixie brought up the subject of Neil. It had been bothering her all afternoon, but she had pushed it to the back of her mind during the visit with Edgar Carver.

"Now I'm sure," she began. "It *was* Neil I saw that day at the filling station, and he wasn't going to Texas. He was coming right here to Cliveden!"

"But how would he have known anything about Rosewood Hall or the necklace?" Di asked innocently. "Didn't you say you told Miss Julie to keep it a secret?"

"Oh, Di, I wish I were as trusting as you are," Trixie said. "Of *course* we pledged her to secrecy, but remember, she's ninety years old. Besides, she adores Neil, and if he got wind of anything we told her, you can bet he'd wheedle the whole story out of her."

"And who knows?" Honey added. "Maybe after we left, more details came back to the old lady, and she told Neil things she didn't even remember when we were there."

"That's a possibility," Trixie said thoughtfully, "but one thing's certain. Neil can't possibly know where the necklace is hidden, because *we* have the diaries and he's never laid eyes on them."

"But now we'll have to be extra careful that he doesn't find out anything more," Jim said. "Maybe we should have warned Mr. Carver about him."

"I thought of that," Trixie said, "but I didn't want to upset him until we knew more about what's up."

"Where do you suppose that Jenkins character fits into the picture?" Brian queried.

"I don't think he fits into *any* picture," Mart replied. "I think he's been a misfit from birth—a real misanthrope, I'd say."

"Well, you *would* say something like that." Trixie laughed. "Come on, now, in plain English, what does misan-something-or-other mean?"

"It's the opposite of philanthropist," Mart answered loftily. "It's someone who hates everybody."

"From that brilliant explanation, I judge a philanthropist is someone who loves everybody," Di said.

"Go to the head of the class," Mart teased.

"Well, to get back to Jenkins," Trixie continued, "I certainly sense something sinister about him."

"Don't let it worry you, Trix," Brian assured her. "We can cope with him if we have to."

With the prospect of their exploration getting under way, everyone was in a gay mood as they returned to the cottage. Mr. and Mrs. Lynch were already there and suggested they all go on the Lanthorn Tour that evening.

"Oh, that'll be fun!" Trixie exclaimed. "It'll keep our minds off—" She stopped, her face reddening as she realized she had almost divulged their secret.

"I have a sneaking suspicion you Bob-Whites are on the trail of another mystery," Mr. Lynch said. "Am I right?"

"Well, maybe," Trixie replied evasively. "They say old houses always have ghosts in them, you know. So who can tell what we might turn up?"

"Then I'll be patient," Di's father said with a laugh. "I've seen how you all work too often to try to get any information out of you. Just be careful you don't get into any trouble."

"Oh, we won't!" Jim reassured him. "Nothing could possibly happen to the Bob-Whites."

As they were approaching Cliveden the next day, Trixie suggested they stop and see Lizzie.

"We can buy some stamps or candy or postcards," she said, "and tell her we saw her old friend."

"From what you and Mr. Carver said, I guess she'd welcome any business," Honey commented, "and besides, I'd love to have a look at her. She sounds a little weird."

"Well, I'll admit that if she had a black cat and a broomstick, she could easily pass for a witch," Trixie replied, "but she's really only kind of pathetic."

Brian, who today was taking his turn driving the station wagon, pulled up in front of the sagging stoop.

"All out and make it snappy," Mart urged them. "I want to get to Green Trees."

There was no sign of life around the place, and as Trixie neared the door, she saw a sign that she was quite sure had not been there before. On a large piece of cardboard, in crude letters, were the words:

KNOCK ON THE DOOR FOR SERVICE. Trixie tried the door and found it locked tight.

"Jeepers! That's funny," she said. "I just walked in before. I wonder what's up?"

"Maybe she's afraid of shoplifters." Mart chuckled. "Although, from your description of her merchandise, I can't imagine who would want to lift anything."

"Go ahead and knock, Trix," Di urged impatiently. "We'll never get to see Lizzie, just standing here."

Trixie gave a loud rap on the door. There was no response, so she knocked again as hard as she could. Then she pressed her nose against one of the small windows in the top of the door. Finally she made out the figure of Lizzie coming around the counter toward the door. The old woman peered out, and Trixie waved her hand, hoping Lizzie would remember her. She apparently did, for she unlocked the door. Poking her head out, she asked suspiciously, "Are all them friends of yours?"

"Yes, Miss James, all friends," Trixie answered. "We need some stamps and postcards and things, and so we thought we'd stop and get them from you. We found the door locked. I hope we didn't disturb you."

Lizzie didn't answer, but she opened the door wide, and they all went in. It was then Trixie noticed that the old woman was carrying a short length of lead pipe.

"Gleeps!" she exclaimed, pretending to draw back in alarm. "What's the matter, Miss James? You look as though you expected a burglar."

"It's worse than that," the old woman replied, locking the door behind her. "It's that Jenkins man. He came around here yesterday with fire in his eye, asking me all sorts of questions about Rosewood Hall, and when I couldn't tell him anything, he got even madder and did this here." She pushed up the sleeve of her dress and revealed an ugly black and blue mark on her arm, where he had grabbed her.

"Oh, what a horrid thing to do!" Trixie exclaimed as the others gathered around. "Whatever did he want to know?"

"He raved on about hidden jewels and was sure I knew something about them," Lizzie explained. "I guess if I knew where there was any hidden treasure, I wouldn't be in *this* miserable town."

"Have you ever heard any such stories?" Trixie asked.

"Oh, yes," Lizzie replied. "Everybody's heard about the lost emeralds, but no one believes they're still at Rosewood. I believe the Yankees stole them, before they burned the house down, along with everything else they could get their hands on."

"Was Jenkins alone when he came in?" Trixie pursued the subject of Jenkins.

"Yes, all alone, and no knowing what he might have done if I hadn't grabbed up a rolling pin from the shelf here and threatened to knock his brains out. You should have seen him run out of here then." The old woman chortled, forgetting her injured arm for

the moment as she thought of how she had bested
Jenkins.

"Well, I think you're wise to keep the door locked,"
Mart said. "I don't suppose you have much of a
constabulary around this town."

"Constabulary!" she hooted. "I should say not, and
the troopers are miles away. Protection! Fiddle-dee-
dee! It's each man for himself."

As the Bob-Whites were picking out some cards
from the rather limited display, Trixie told Lizzie
how they had visited Green Trees and met Mr.
Carver.

"He's a real gentleman, he is," the old lady said
with a shake of her head, "and never a complaint
about being so lame and all. You know, he's one
person who hasn't got an enemy in the whole world!"

"Does he live all by himself?" Trixie asked.

"All soul alone," was the answer. "He has someone
come in once a week or so to do the heavy cleaning,
but he's learned to manage for himself. I'm right
pleased you had a chance to meet him."

"So are we," Trixie said. "We'll never forget Green
Trees or Mr. Carver."

After they had made their purchases, they bade
good-bye to Lizzie, promising they would stop again
if they had time before going home.

"Well, what do you think of *that?*" Trixie asked
when they were outside. "It looks as though our
friend Jenkins is in on the secret, too!"

"That's probably why he chased us off when we

were poking around the ruins," Brian commented.

"And I'll bet he's the one who had been digging around there before we arrived on the scene," Trixie said.

As they drove past Rosewood, they all craned their necks to see if there was any sign of Neil or Jenkins, but the place looked as deserted as it had before.

"Let's leave the station wagon on the far side of the house when we get to Green Trees," Trixie suggested. "It won't be as conspicuous there."

"Then you really think they're spying on us?" Di asked.

"Well, I certainly wouldn't put it past them," Mart replied.

"I'm sure of it," Trixie agreed, "and I wish the cemetery weren't so close to Jenkins's line. If they see us in there, they'll certainly be suspicious that we're on the trail of something."

After they had parked the car, they walked around the house toward Mr. Carver's study. They found him outside on the terrace, with a sketch pad on his lap. He greeted them cordially and, after showing them the drawings he was working on, said, "The key to the family vault is on the desk inside. I only hope you're not embarking on a wild-goose chase."

"I hope so, too," Trixie sighed. "I'll simply die if we don't find the clue. Right now I must admit I can't imagine where Ruth could have hidden it." She started into the house to get the key, leaving the others to talk with Mr. Carver.

"I wish I could offer you Bob-Whites some suggestions," he said, "but I haven't been inside the mausoleum for many years, and my memory of it is very foggy. I have only a vague impression of a somber, dimly lit room, nothing more."

"Well, knowing Trixie as I do," Jim said, "if the message is there, she'll find it."

"What's that you're saying behind my back?" Trixie asked with pretended petulance as she returned with the key.

"Oh, you were just getting another compliment from your not-so-secret admirer," Mart quipped.

"Oh, skip it!" Trixie cried, red-faced, giving her brother a shove. Then, immediately feeling ashamed at her show of temper in front of Mr. Carver, she added, "I'm sorry, sir, but brothers can be *such* pests! But to get back to our project, don't you think it would be a good idea for us to go around the back way through the gardens, instead of across the lawn? We wouldn't be nearly as conspicuous."

"I may have an even better idea," Brian said. "I think you and Jim ought to go by yourselves, Trixie. Two won't be as noticeable as six of us, if anyone *is* on the lookout for us. Here's the 'open sesame.'" He took the can of penetrating oil from his pocket and tossed it to Jim.

"You mean you think you're being spied on?" Mr. Carver asked in surprise.

When Trixie told him about Neil and how she had seen him the previous day, and about Lizzie's encounter with Jenkins, Mr. Carver whistled softly.

"I had no idea this thing was assuming such proportions," he said. "I wonder, really, whether you ought to go on with your search. I would never forgive myself if anything should happen to you."

"Oh, nothing is going to happen," Trixie said with forced cheerfulness. "Jenkins is obviously a cowardly character, or he wouldn't have run away from Lizzie and her rolling pin."

"And we can certainly cope with Neil if we have to," Jim added. "We've handled his kind before, haven't we, Trixie?"

"We certainly have. Remember Slim at Cobbett's Island?"

"How could I ever forget!" Jim laughed as he told Mr. Carver of their encounter in the stable of the Oldest House.

"Well, you and Jim see what luck you have," Mr. Carver said to Trixie, "and if you run into any kind of trouble, you call out."

"Oh, we have our own danger signal," Trixie assured him. "Listen!" She gave the Bob-White whistle, which Jim had taught them when the club was first organized.

"That's the best imitation of the quail's call I've ever heard." Mr. Carver laughed. "It would fool anyone. Now, I think you'd better get started. From the looks of those clouds, we may be in for a storm."

Jim and Trixie started around the rear of the house and down a long alley of boxwood that had grown so high through the years that it hid them completely. This path ended in a formal garden much like those they had seen in Williamsburg. Beyond it was the grove of cryptomerias. They skirted the side of the garden, bending low so as to be as unobtrusive as possible, and finally came to the burying ground. It was a small plot, enclosed by an ornate iron fence. The gate was ajar, and, going through it, Trixie and Jim saw rows of moss-covered headstones. In the rear was a small but impressive marble mausoleum. Climbing the wide steps of the structure, Trixie approached the great double door and inserted the key in the lock.

"Keep your fingers crossed," she said as she tried to turn it. Despite her best efforts, it wouldn't budge. Jim attempted to turn it, with no success.

"I guess we'd better try Brian's suggestion and not waste any more time," he said, taking the can of oil from his pocket. He squirted a generous amount into the keyhole and stood back. "We'll let this work for a few minutes and see if it's as good as he claims."

"While we're waiting, let's look at some of those stones out there," Trixie said as she led the way down one of the narrow paths. They stopped to read the old inscriptions. "Look, Jim, here's one with the dates 1746 to 1749 on it. A child's grave. Ooooh! Cemeteries give me the shivers!"

The sky was growing steadily darker, and soon large drops of rain began to fall. A sudden clap of thunder made them both jump, and they hurried back to the vault to get out of the rain.

"Let's hope we can get inside, or we'll be soaked," Jim said as he tried the lock again. Fortunately, the oil had done the job, and the heavy bolt slid back as the key turned, allowing them to push open the massive door. By now the rain was teeming, and the inside of the mausoleum was pitch black, but at least, they consoled themselves, they were out of the storm.

The Clue Ruth Left · 10

THE RAIN will soon let up," Jim assured her, once they were inside the vault. "You know what Shakespeare said: 'Small showers last long, but sudden storms are short.'"

"I hope old Will was right!" Trixie exclaimed. She felt a shiver run up her spine as she took a few wary steps into the dark. She was thankful Jim had left the door ajar and was close by to bolster her courage.

"Jeepers! This place gives me the creeps," she said. "Now I know what they mean when they say 'cold as the tomb'!"

"It's eerie, all right," Jim agreed, "but there's really nothing to fear."

"You hope!" Trixie added, wrapping her arms tightly around herself.

As a flash of lightning momentarily lit up the room, she caught a glimpse of two benches along the wall.

Her knees were shaking, and she was glad to sit down and pull herself together. Jim joined her, and for a few minutes they were silent, listening to the storm raging outside and trying to accustom their eyes to the darkness.

"Sssssh," Jim whispered suddenly. "Do you hear anything odd out there?"

Trixie cocked her head and listened intently.

"Nothing special, Jim," she answered. "I think it's the wind in the trees, but I must admit I have a strange feeling of danger."

"It's probably just our imaginations. The atmosphere of this place makes us jumpy," Jim said, getting up and walking toward the door to look out. "I *hope* it's only the wind. I wouldn't welcome any intruders, until we have a chance to see what's here."

"Have you any idea about where we might start?" Trixie tried to keep her voice light, despite her uneasiness.

"I can't say I have," Jim replied. "I was counting on you, as usual, for inspiration."

"Well, at the moment, I confess I haven't a single idea," Trixie said. "Suppose we try doing what the little boy did when he lost his horse."

"What was that?" Jim asked. "I don't think I've ever heard that."

"His father asked him how he'd found his pet horse, and the little boy said, 'I just thought to myself, *Where would I go if I was a horse?* and I went, and he *had!*'"

"Fair enough!" Jim chuckled. "Okay, then, if you were going to hide a secret message, where would you put it?"

"Since we know it's somewhere in the cemetery, I think I'd put it under a stone," Trixie said.

"There's only one trouble with that theory," Jim commented. "Those stones out there would be much too heavy for one person to lift. No, I'm afraid you'll have to try again, old girl."

"I suppose you're right." Trixie sighed. "How about someplace in here? It would be more protected than outside in the weather."

"That makes sense," Jim said. "By the way, the rain seems to be letting up. It's getting lighter all of a sudden."

The fact that the little building had no windows added to the murkiness of the place, but the details of the room gradually emerged as the clouds began to break up. The rear wall was paneled with large marble slabs inscribed with the names and dates of burial of members of the Carver and Fields families. It was apparent that the smooth surface offered no possible hiding place for whatever Ruth had hidden. They turned their attention to the other parts of the room. With Jim's help, Trixie lifted the stone benches to be sure there was nothing underneath. Next, they went over every inch of the floor, looking for loose stones. There were none. The floor was cold, smooth marble.

"You know, Jim," Trixie said, sitting down on one

of the benches again and pushing the damp curls from her forehead, "I'd rather look for a needle in a haystack than try to find anything in this place. I'm ready to give up!"

She threw up her hands in desperation, and, as she looked up at Jim, her eyes carried beyond him. She noticed for the first time two arched niches, high up in the wall—too high, in fact, for either of them to reach.

"Look, Jim!" she cried, jumping to her feet. "Up in that little cubbyhole. See that vase?"

"Sure, I see it. It's as plain as my nose, now that you mention it," he said. Then, pointing to the niche on the other side of the door, he added, "I wonder why that one is empty."

"It *is* queer," Trixie replied. "Come to think of it, that urn is the only thing in here that isn't balanced— two benches, two doors, two sconces for candles. I wonder why."

"Maybe the other vase got broken," Jim suggested.

"Mmmmm, could be," Trixie mused, "but I don't think so. I have a hunch that having only one may have been deliberate. I'll bet Ruth put it up there, knowing that it would be conspicuous to anyone hunting for the message. Here, boost me up, Jim. I've got to take a look inside that urn!"

Jim made a cradle of his hands, and Trixie, kicking off her loafers, stepped up and was just able to reach the niche and hold on to the edge with one hand.

"Oh, Jim—it's just got to be in here!" she said

breathlessly. She took careful hold of the vase and
tucked it under her arm. "Easy, now. Let me down,"
she said, almost in a whisper.

She put the beautiful little porcelain urn on the
bench, reached inside, and drew out a small red
velvet bag. She didn't say a word as she untied the
drawstring and took out a heavy gold locket in the
shape of a heart.

"Jim," she said urgently, "there's something en-
graved on the face of it. Let's go over by the door.
It's too dark back here to make it out."

Quickly she stepped across the little room. Then,
catching the light over her shoulder, she read, slowly
and distinctly, " 'To RSF, with love. Christmas,
1861.' "

"Open it, Trix," Jim whispered. "This is it—the
clue Ruth left for Helen!"

"Oh, Jim," Trixie moaned, "you try it. My fingers
are all thumbs. I can't manage it!"

Jim took the locket from her shaking hands, and in
a moment he had discovered the secret—a little knob
on the side of the locket, which, when pressed, re-
leased the hidden lock. It opened easily, and without
saying anything, he handed it back to Trixie.

There were two sections in the locket, the one in
front holding a picture of a young man and woman.
In the middle frame was a delicately woven ring of
hair, mingled dark brown and gold.

"That must be Ruth and her husband," Trixie said,
looking intently at the faded picture. "RSF stands

for Ruth Sunderland Fields—and look, Jim! She's wearing a necklace! I'll bet it's the emeralds!"

When she turned to the back part of the locket, she saw, in the space where ordinarily there would have been another picture, a small bit of folded paper. She was about to take it out, when a shadow fell across the door and the silence was shattered!

"Okay, you grave robbers! Hand it over!"

"Jim! It's Neil!" Trixie shouted. She clutched the locket tightly in her hand. "Get him out of here!"

"Oh, no, you don't!" the boy cried, lunging toward Jim, and before Trixie knew what was happening, the two were grappling, each trying to push the other far enough away to land a blow. Neil was about the same height as Jim, and, while he wasn't quite as heavy, he was wiry and strong. Trixie watched spellbound for a minute or two, and then, fearing that Jim might be in trouble, she dashed outside. Running a few steps toward the house, she gave the Bob-White whistle loud and clear, repeating it several times in the hope that it would bring help—and quickly.

When she got back to the mausoleum, Jim and Neil were still fighting savagely. Neil freed himself just long enough to level a blow at Jim's head, but Jim saw it coming and ducked in time to avoid it. Then, seeing Neil off-balance, Jim dealt him a thumping wallop on the shoulder that sent him spinning around and down. Too late, Trixie tried to grab the urn from the bench. As Neil sprawled over the seat, the beautiful vase shattered.

"Now, get going!" Jim barked as Neil pulled himself slowly to his feet and sidled past them. Without a backward glance, the boy ran through the cemetery, jumped the fence, and made off in the direction of Rosewood Hall. At the same time, Trixie saw the Bob-Whites racing toward her. Seeing Neil, they were about to follow him, but Trixie signaled for them to come to her.

Turning her attention to Jim, she asked, "Are you all right?"

"I seem to be all in one piece," he said, shaking his head and bending his legs. "Nothing hurts, but I'm sure winded!"

"What's the idea, Trix?" Brian asked. "That was Neil, wasn't it? We could easily have caught him."

"I know you could," Trixie answered, slipping into her loafers, "but I think he may be more valuable to us if we let him go this time. It's Jenkins we should worry about more than Neil."

"How do you figure that?" Honey asked. "It seems to me Neil's the one who has been acting suspiciously all along."

"I know, I know," Trixie said, an edge of impatience in her voice. "It looks as though he were up to no good, I'll admit, but for the time being I'm giving him the benefit of the doubt."

"But *why?*" Mart asked. "I don't think you're being your usual logical self, dear sister."

"It's not a matter of logic," Trixie said, too engrossed in the analysis of her own feelings to resent

Mart's criticism. "It's more a *feeling* I have about Neil." She paused, trying to find words to express herself. "I don't like him, and yet—"

"You've obviously got ambivalent feelings about him," Mart interrupted, and he nodded his head very knowingly.

"What kind of feelings?" Di asked. "Are you pulling another of your gags, Mart? Come on; be serious."

"I'm perfectly serious," Mart answered with a straight face. "Ambivalent feelings are when you feel two ways about something or someone at the same time. Am I right, Trix?"

"For once, dear brother, you've hit the nail on the head," Trixie said. "Let's start back to the house, and I'll tell you what I mean."

As they started up the path toward the garden, Trixie continued, "I think Neil has a gentle side to his nature, and that's why he took such good care of Miss Julie. On the other hand, he probably heard about the emeralds and figured he'd try to get to Rosewood Hall and take a chance on finding them."

"Miss Julie may have told him the same thing she told us," Honey said. "Remember the day we were there, Trix? She said she never had liked jewelry, and she obviously wasn't interested in having the emeralds, no matter how valuable they are."

"You're right," Trixie said, "and I'll never forget how proud she looked when she told us she was 'comfortably off.' Neil probably felt that he had just as much right to hunt for the treasure as we did."

"Well, I follow you so far," Jim said, "but what about his sneaking around Green Trees? How do you explain that?"

"I was just coming to that," Trixie answered. "Maybe when he found out about Mr. Carver being a cripple, he felt sympathetic toward him the way he did toward Miss Julie, and that day he saw the cars in the driveway, he may have just been checking up to see if Mr. Carver was all right."

"If that's true, then what about today?" Mart asked impatiently. "What was he doing breaking in on you and Jim that way?"

"He could really have thought we were stealing something from the mausoleum," Trixie replied. "He called us 'grave robbers,' you know."

"Everything is 'maybe,'" Brian cut in, "pure conjecture. I still don't see why, if Neil is so interested in Mr. Carver, he didn't go call on him and get to know him."

"You've got a point there, all right," Trixie mused. "I don't see why, either, unless he felt he would have to give up the emeralds if he found them. I'm confused! Don't think I'm not! Let's get on back to the house and talk to Mr. Carver about it."

As they approached Green Trees, they saw Edgar Carver slowly propelling his wheelchair down the garden path toward them, a worried look on his handsome face. Trixie called out to him that they were all right.

"I began to be worried," he said as the Bob-Whites

came up. "I decided I'd better get down there and have a look, but it's rather slow going in this thing."

"I'll push you back to the house, and Trixie can tell you all about it," Jim said, carefully turning the wheelchair around and heading back toward the house.

"Well, I'll admit we had kind of a close call," Trixie said. "Just as we found the locket, Neil came in, and, before I could read the paper in it, we almost lost it— But there I go again," she laughed, "getting the cart before the horse, as I always do!"

"Neil? A locket? This all sounds very mysterious," Mr. Carver said. "Push me up that ramp at the end of the terrace, Jim." He smiled. "Then we can all sit down and relax. In the meantime, Trixie can collect her thoughts so she can tell me what did happen."

As soon as they had gathered in the study, Trixie gave the locket to Mr. Carver, telling him how she had found it in the urn.

"Have you ever seen it before?" she asked. "Do you think it was Ruth's?" Her eyes were bright with excitement.

Mr. Carver cradled the locket in his hand, looking first at the initials on the front and then opening it and gazing at the picture of the two young people.

"I have no doubt it is Ruth and Lee. There is a striking resemblance between her and my mother— the same deep-set eyes and wide brow."

"Now look in the back," Trixie urged him. "There's

the paper I started to tell you about. We never had a chance to read it, because Neil came in just at that moment and tried to get it away from us."

"Who is this Neil?" Mr. Carver asked. "I don't think I've ever heard that name, and I know almost everyone around here."

"Well, it's a strange coincidence"—Jim took up the story—"but this boy, who apparently is working at Rosewood Hall—well, he's the same one Trixie and Honey met when they were talking with Miss Julie Sunderland in Croton."

"It doesn't sound like a coincidence to me," Mr. Carver replied. "Don't you think he might be down here for the same reason you are?"

"That's what *I* think," Trixie said, "but we can't be sure, even though it looks awfully suspicious."

"Trixie thinks we should sort of watch and wait before we accuse him of having any ulterior motives," Mart said.

"That's probably wise," Mr. Carver agreed, "but if he's connected with Jenkins in any way, I'd be on my guard. Now, let's take a look at this paper. I can see that Trixie, at the moment, is more interested in it than she is in Jenkins."

"Does my curiosity show that plainly?" Trixie asked.

"I'm afraid it does, my dear," he replied with a warm smile, "so you read it right now and see if it's what you've been looking for so diligently."

He handed the heart back to Trixie, who carefully

removed the little square of paper from under the glass of the locket. There wasn't a sound in the library as she unfolded it and read aloud. "'Look in the secret passage between the Twin Houses, behind a brick marked with an X. May the charm of the necklace bring only good luck.'"

All eyes turned to Mr. Carver, who sat as though stunned. Finally, looking up, he said, "Oh, Trixie, I hate to tell you this, but *I've* never heard of any secret passage between Rosewood Hall and Green Trees!"

A Bad Blow · 11

THE COLOR drained out of Trixie's face, and the only sound was the sharp intake of her breath and a low "Oh, no!" She walked slowly over to the sofa and sat down between Jim and Honey.

Edgar Carver, perceiving how crushed she was, rolled his chair over to her as her brothers and Di gathered close around the divan.

"Take heart, Trixie," Mr. Carver said. "The fact that *I* am ignorant of any such passage doesn't mean there isn't one."

"But certainly you would have heard about it, wouldn't you?" Trixie asked despairingly.

"Not necessarily," he answered. "You see, after the untimely death of my mother and father, I was raised by a succession of nurses and governesses who were hired by the executors of my father's estate. The chances are that they would not have known anything about any such secret passage. And I was much too young to remember anything about it, even if I had been told by my father."

"And you haven't *any* idea where it might be?" Trixie asked, grasping at straws.

"I'm sorry, I don't, but that doesn't mean we can't find it." Mr. Carver was obviously trying to encourage her. "With all the Bob-Whites to help you," he went on, almost tenderly, "and with your own talent for solving knotty problems, I'm sure you can work this one out, too."

The others tried to be just as reassuring, and it wasn't long before Trixie, taking a deep breath, stood up and said in a confident voice, "All right. I'll try, but we've just got to find something specific to work on."

"Such as?" Mart asked earnestly.

"That's a good question," Trixie said ruefully. She thought a long minute and then went on. "Maybe if we go over all the facts we already have, something will occur to us. First, we have to assume there *is* a passage between the two houses, and, since it's nowhere above the ground, it must be a tunnel. Right?"

"Right!" Honey echoed. "And it must start on the side of Green Trees nearest Rosewood Hall. That would be this side of the house, and it would end up over there on the left, where Rosewood stood."

"Elementary, my dear Watson," Jim chuckled. "And the chances are, its being a tunnel, that it is reached via the cellar, wouldn't you say?"

"Another brilliant deduction, Jim." Brian applauded weakly.

"Well, Green Trees has a cellar, all right," Mr. Carver contributed, "but, you know, I've never in my whole life been in it. Perhaps you should have a look, although I know that when the house was being restored, the cellar was gone over very carefully. They wanted to be sure there weren't any weak places in the foundations."

"They might have overlooked the entrance to the passage if it were concealed in any way," Trixie said thoughtfully. "We've got to examine every inch of it. Do you think the historical society would mind, Mr. Carver?"

"I'm sure they wouldn't," he assured her. "As a matter of fact, the floor plans of the house, which they drew up, might be of some help to you."

"Gleeps!" Trixie exclaimed. "Things are suddenly looking up again. Could we see them—the plans, I mean? We'll be going home in three days, you know, so we can't waste a minute."

"It's a bit late today," Mr. Carver reflected, glancing at his watch. "However, I'll phone Miss Bates—she's the head of the historical society—and see if she can come over tomorrow. We can tell her you suspect there is a passage between the two houses, but, for the time being, we won't say anything about the necklace. It seems best to keep that to ourselves until we've gone a little further with this investigation."

"Jeepers!" Trixie cried. "I don't think I'll be able to wait until tomorrow to explore the cellar, but you're right, Mr. Carver; it's getting late, and Di's parents will begin to wonder what's keeping us so long. I'll try to be patient, for once in my life!"

"Well, come as early in the morning as you like." Mr. Carver smiled as they called out their farewells. "I always wake up with the birds."

There was no one in sight at Rosewood Hall as the Bob-Whites passed by it on their way back to Williamsburg.

"I'd sure like to know what goes on in there," Mart said, looking down the driveway. "I wonder if Neil and Jenkins are doing any more digging in the ruins? You know, it could be they might stumble on the passage before we find it. And if *that* happened *they* could just as easily find the X-marked brick."

"Don't think I haven't thought of that," Trixie moaned. "I'll *die* if we don't discover it tomorrow!"

The Bob-Whites decided they should tell Mr. and Mrs. Lynch something about their search for the passage. "It isn't fair not to let them know why we are continually running out to Green Trees," Trixie said.

"You're right," Di agreed. "Daddy and Mummy have been marvelous about letting us go on our own, but I'd feel better, too, if they were in on at least part of the mystery."

"The idea of a charmed necklace might seem so

preposterous to them," Jim said, "that I agree with
Mr. Carver. We'd better keep that under our hats
for a while."

That evening at dinner, Trixie told Mr. and Mrs.
Lynch about finding the locket in the cemetery,
taking it to Edgar Carver, and discovering the
reference to a secret passage.

"So that's what's been occupying you young folks!"
Mr. Lynch said when she finished. "I must admit I
was on the point of asking what you had all been so
busy about, but Mother, here, reminded me you
were old enough to keep out of trouble, so I didn't
interfere."

"You've been wonderful, Mr. Lynch," Trixie said.
"It's really been exciting, and if we can only find the
passage, there's no knowing what it might lead to."

"These old houses are often full of surprises," Mr.
Lynch said. "Why, just the other day I heard of one
with a secret room that no one knew existed, until a
wall was torn out in the process of remodeling."

"Did they find anything exciting in it?" Di asked
her father.

"No, not a thing." He laughed. "It was as empty
as the proverbial drum."

"Well," Trixie said, "I hope tomorrow we'll be able
to find the passage without having to tear out any
walls."

"I wish you luck," Mr. Lynch said. "Don't forget,
we plan to leave for home day after tomorrow, so you
don't have very much time."

"Oh, I know," Trixie sighed, "but Mr. Carver told us we could come out as early as we like in the morning, so we'll have the whole day."

"We could take lunch with us," Mart suggested, "and, if the weather's good, eat out in the garden."

"Trust Mart to remember the food detail!" Di laughed. "But, actually, it's a good idea. Mart won't be the only hungry one in the crowd, I know."

"I'll have some box lunches packed for you here at the restaurant," Mrs. Lynch volunteered. "You can pick them up after you've had breakfast."

"Oh, wonderful, Mummy!" Di exclaimed. "And please order an extra one for Mr. Carver. He's been so kind to us. Then we can all eat together."

Trixie awoke almost before dawn the next morning, but she didn't waken Di or Honey right away. She lay in bed, her head cradled in her arms, mulling over the events of the last few days to see if there were any loose threads she had overlooked. She recalled what Mart had said the previous day about the possibility of Jenkins and Neil stumbling on the passage on the Rosewood side, and the idea made her almost sick with apprehension.

"I've *got* to find out what's going on over there," she thought to herself, "but *how?*"

She could think of no way to revisit Rosewood without being accused of trespassing. And Jenkins was no one she wanted to risk angering again. "At least," she consoled herself, "even though he and

Neil may know about the necklace, they don't know
where it's hidden. They must still be searching in
the dark, if they're searching at all—"

Her reflections were interrupted by Honey calling
softly to her from her bed.

"Di never seems to let anything interfere with her
beauty sleep, does she? I'll bet she'd sleep till eleven,
if we didn't get her up. How long have you been
awake, Trix?"

"Practically the whole night!" Trixie said wryly.
"My mind has been spinning like a top."

"Mine, too," Honey said, "but I can't say I came to
any earthshaking conclusions. How about you?"

"I didn't, either," Trixie answered. "Let's start to
wake Di up. You know how long it takes her to get
going in the morning."

By the time the girls had showered and dressed,
they heard the boys outside and went to join them.

"Do you think it's too early to start out?" Jim asked
Trixie.

"Oh, by the time we have breakfast and pick up the
box lunches and drive out there, it'll be close to nine
o'clock," Trixie replied. "I think that's okay, don't
you?" She looked at the others to see how they felt.

"Sure, it's okay," Mart agreed. "Let's not waste
time talking about it. We've got work to do!"

They all shared Mart's sense of excitement and
expectancy as they drove toward Cliveden. Because
of the early hour, they decided against stopping to
see Lizzie James this trip.

As they drove into the Green Trees driveway, Trixie suddenly seized Jim's arm. "Look!" she cried. "Over there beyond the terrace! That man on horse-back—isn't it Jenkins?"

"It sure is, Trix," Brian agreed. "And look at him beating that poor animal! Why on earth is he in such a hurry to get back to Rosewood?"

Jim slammed on the brakes, and they all piled out of the car and started around the house toward Mr. Carver's study. Trixie, who had been in the front seat, got a head start and was the first to reach the French doors. Sensing something was wrong, she raced inside. What she saw made her heart miss a beat. On the floor, beside the large mahogany desk, lay Mr. Carver, his forehead covered with blood. His legs were thrust out at an unnatural angle from the wheelchair, which was lying on its side, the back completely broken away from the seat.

Jim and Brian, who were close behind Trixie, rushed around the desk and knelt beside the fallen man. From the looks on their faces, Trixie knew the situation was serious. She motioned the others to stay back until Brian had had a chance to examine the injured man.

"Trix, bring me some clean cloths and water. Quick!" Brian ordered tensely. "And you, Mart, come and help Jim get this broken chair out of the way."

At first Trixie couldn't think where to look for water and cloths, but suddenly she remembered seeing a small sink in Mr. Carver's studio. She ran

into the solarium, washed out a small pitcher she
found on a shelf near the sink, filled it, and quickly
grabbed up some cloths he apparently kept for cleaning his brushes.

"Good girl," Brian said when she returned. "These
aren't sterile, but they'll do to get the worst of the
blood cleaned up, so we can see how much damage
has been done."

By this time, Mart and Jim had succeeded in extri-
cating the wheelchair, and after Brian had assured
himself that none of Mr. Carver's bones were broken,
they lifted the unconscious man onto the sofa and
covered him gently with his lap robe.

"He got a bad blow when he fell, but his pulse is
pretty good, and so is his respiration. We want to
keep his head elevated a little, in case he may have
a concussion." Brian adjusted the pillows on the sofa
with professional skill.

"Do *you* think it was the fall that hurt him?"
Honey whispered to Trixie. "Or did Jenkins hit him?"

"I'm pretty sure he struck his head as he fell,"
Trixie answered under her breath, at the same time
drawing Honey aside, toward the desk. "I noticed
traces of blood on the corner of the desk here, just
where he would have fallen."

"You're wonderful, Trix!" Honey said as they re-
joined the others. "Even in an emergency, you keep
your head level and your eyes open."

When Brian had finally cleaned the wound as best
he could, he took a freshly laundered handkerchief

from his pocket and flipped it open, being careful not to touch the part that would come in contact with the ugly abrasion on Mr. Carver's forehead.

"This is the closest thing to a sterile dressing I can manage," he explained as he deftly adjusted the makeshift bandage. "Ironing half sterilizes cloth, and I folded it as carefully as I could."

Honey had been following Brian's every move, as had the others, but at the same time, she had seen to it that Mr. Carver was kept covered. Trixie smiled inwardly, for she well remembered how her friend used to quail at the sight of blood. Now Honey seemed just as able to help in an emergency as any other Bob-White.

As a matter of fact, Trixie thought, *I'll bet she'd make a first-rate nurse, as well as a detective.*

Di and Mart, in the meantime, had been sponging up the spot on the floor and getting things in order again. It was not too long before Mr. Carver began to respond. His eyes slowly opened, and he looked around as though not quite sure of his whereabouts. Then, seeing the Bob-Whites nearby, he smiled weakly and tried to raise his head.

"You had an accident, sir," Brian told him, "but you'll be all right. Just try to relax and lie still."

"What happened?" the man asked weakly, putting his hand to his brow. "My head is splitting."

It was on the tip of Trixie's tongue to tell him about seeing Jenkins riding from the house, but she decided against it. It would be better to wait until

he had had a chance to regain his strength before
attempting to find out just what had happened.

"You fell out of your wheelchair," she said, "and
it looks as though you gave yourself a terrific knock
on the edge of the desk."

"I don't understand it," Mr. Carver answered. "I've
never had an accident in all the years I've been using
it. I don't understand!"

"Don't try to figure it out just now," Brian urged
him. "I think the thing for us to do at the moment
is to get a doctor to look at your head and put on a
proper dressing. The one I fixed up is pretty inade-
quate, I'm afraid."

"You *do* have a doctor, don't you?" Trixie asked
solicitously.

"Yes, there's Alex, though I think of him more as
my friend than as my doctor." Mr. Carver paused
as though speaking tired him. "Except for my legs,
I am remarkably fit, but Alex drops over every so
often for a game of chess. He was here last evening,
as a matter of fact."

"May we call him?" Trixie asked. "We want to be
sure you're all right."

"If it will make you feel easier," he said with a faint
smile. "I'll admit my head could use relief of some
kind. Look in the directory on my desk. He's listed
there under Alexander Brandon."

Trixie went to the desk and, having found the
number, put in a call for the doctor. As she waited
for the nurse to locate him, she glanced over Mr.

Carver's neatly kept desk. Suddenly she noticed, far over on one side, almost hidden by a newspaper, the gold locket. It was open, and when she reached over and took it in her hand, her heart almost stopped beating. The little piece of paper—the directions for finding the necklace—was missing!

"Of course, he might have put it away for safe-keeping," she told herself frantically. "But why hadn't he put the locket away, too?" That he would have just flung it to one side of the desk didn't fit in with his apparent orderliness. "No," she conjectured, "Jenkins has been here!"

Jim must have sensed that Trixie was deeply disturbed, because he stepped over to her side. Just then Dr. Brandon came on the phone. All Trixie had time to do was to place the open locket in Jim's hand. He let out a low whistle and quickly slipped it into the desk drawer.

When Trixie told the doctor about Mr. Carver's wound and severe headache, he voiced concern and said he would come to Green Trees immediately. In answer to his question, Trixie told him who she was and started explaining how she had happened to be on hand, but he cut her short.

"Oh, yes," he said, "Edgar told me about you all last evening. I can't tell you how fortunate it is you arrived when you did. Now, keep him warm, and see that his head is elevated a little. It shouldn't take me more than a few minutes to get there."

An Unlikely Friend · 12

IT PROBABLY was only a few minutes, but to Trixie it seemed like hours before she heard a car come up the driveway and, looking out, saw a tall, well-built man stride rapidly toward the house and up to the terrace door. Except for hurried introductions and a word or two of reassurance to Edgar Carver, Dr. Brandon lost no time before going about the business of examining his friend.

"It might be a good idea for you girls to make some hot tea," he said as he pulled up a chair beside the sofa. "The kitchen is at the end of the hall, beyond the studio. In the meantime, we'll finish getting Edgar bandaged up and see if we can't relieve his headache."

As Trixie, Di, and Honey went into the kitchen, they thought at first they had made a mistake and were in the wrong room. It was unlike any kitchen they had ever seen. There were no wall cabinets above the working surfaces, and the sink and stove were unusually low, but Trixie almost immediately came up with the explanation for this unorthodox arrangement.

"It's designed so Mr. Carver can reach everything he needs from his wheelchair," she exclaimed. "What a clever idea!"

It didn't take Honey long to find the teakettle and fill it with water. The kitchen was neat as a pin, the tea things arranged on a low shelf near the stove for easy access.

"What can I do to help?" Trixie asked. "You know me and a kitchen. I'm helpless!"

Di, who was already busy putting extra cups and saucers on a tray, said, "Why wouldn't it be a good idea to get the sandwiches from the box lunches to serve with the tea? It's not lunchtime yet, I know, but we've had so much excitement, I think everyone might like a bite to eat."

"You can be sure Mart will." Honey laughed. "It's a good idea, Di. How about getting the boxes from the station wagon for us, Trixie?"

"That sounds like an assignment I could manage."

Noticing that the kitchen door led out to the driveway, she used it so she would not disturb the doctor and Mr. Carver. She was rounding the corner of the house, when she heard a voice call to her.

"Hey! Trixie!"

She spun around and found herself face-to-face

with Neil, who apparently had been hiding behind a tall clump of bushes. His face was white, the expression in his eyes was worried, and, as he approached her, his shoulders were hunched and he was wringing his hands nervously. Trixie was about to ask him what he was doing there, but something in his manner made her wait to let him speak first.

"Is he all right?" Neil asked. "Jenkins mentioned an accident. He's not hurt bad, is he?"

Trixie was dumbfounded. Her amazement must have shown on her face, because before she had time to answer, Neil went on, "Please say he's all right. I can't stand any more cruelty."

"I don't think he's badly hurt," Trixie said. "What did Mr. Jenkins tell you? Mr. Carver thinks he fell out of his wheelchair, but I have other ideas."

"You mean," Neil asked incredulously, "he doesn't remember anything?"

"That's right," Trixie answered sharply. "His mind seems to be a complete blank about the fall."

"I wish I could tell you what happened, Trixie, honest I do!" The boy's face was wretched. "All Jenkins said was there had been an accident. If I can get anything more out of him, I'll tell you, I promise. I want to talk with you, Trixie. I want you to know why I came down here and all. Please give me a chance."

"I'd like to talk to you, too, Neil," Trixie said, her voice softening a little. "Right now I've got to get some things out of the station wagon and go back to the house, but if you're serious, and I think you are, I'll come back as soon as I can. You wait here." And she was off.

He was still there when she returned with the lunch boxes, and, as she passed him, she said, "I'll make it as fast as I can. You just stay put."

When she, Di, and Honey got back to the library with the tea tray and sandwiches, they found Dr. Brandon talking with Brian about Mr. Carver's head.

"I'm pretty certain there's no concussion," he said, "but I want to be absolutely sure, and an X ray is the best way to check."

"Oh, come, now, Alex, you're making a mountain out of a molehill," Edgar Carver chided his friend. "My head's beginning to feel better already. I even think I could drink a cup of tea."

"No, I won't let you talk me out of it," Dr. Brandon replied. "You've had your way too long about that operation I want you to have, so now it's *my* turn to be stubborn."

Trixie was immediately attentive. "An operation?" she asked, turning to the doctor.

Dr. Brandon glanced at his friend, who, with a slight wave of his hand, indicated that it would be all right if he answered Trixie's question.

"Well, when Mr. Carver was a little boy— You weren't more than five or six, were you?" he asked, looking at the other man, who nodded almost imperceptibly. "He fell downstairs on Christmas morning, injuring his back so that he lost the use of his legs."

"How dreadfull" Trixie cried. "Couldn't anything be done?"

"We're not sure what steps were taken at the time," the doctor went on, "and it's useless to try to fix the blame for things that happened so long ago, but I have reason to think it's not too late to do something about it. Medical science has made tremendous strides since then."

"And you don't favor an operation, Mr. Carver?" Brian asked solicitously.

Mr. Carver was silent for a minute before he answered, and then, with a smile at the doctor, he said, "I've learned to get along very well over the years, and I. . . ." His voice trailed off into silence.

"Come, now," Dr. Brandon said, laying a hand gently on Edgar Carver's shoulder. "I don't want to upset you after the shock you've had this morning. Let's just say your refusal is a matter of pride. I think your young friends here will understand."

"Indeed we do!" Trixie spoke for all of them. "But wouldn't it be wonderful if something *could* be done?"

"It certainly would!" the doctor replied earnestly. "But now, Brian, to get back to more immediate problems. I noticed, didn't I, that you came down in a station wagon? Would it be possible for you to drive Edgar to my office? I have an X-ray machine there, and it would save a good deal of time."

"Of course we can," Brian said, jumping to his feet. "We'll put the backseats down and fix up a comfortable place for Mr. Carver to lie; he won't have to sit up at all. Come on, Jim, and you, too, Mart. Take out some of those pillows and that afghan over there on the chair, and as soon as we have everything ready, we'll be back to carry Mr. Carver out."

"Well, I guess I'm outnumbered," said the invalid with a smile. "You win!"

"We'll stay here and clean up the tea things," Honey said as she began gathering up the empty cups and plates. "Good luck, Mr. Carver, and don't you worry about a thing!"

Trixie had already left the room, and when Di and Honey got to the kitchen, they were surprised not to find her there.

"I wonder where she could have gone," Di said, frowning. "It isn't like her to run off without telling us where she's going."

"She probably went to help the boys," Honey answered mildly. "You know she'd much rather do something like that than wash dishes. Don't worry. She'll be back soon."

Trixie had guessed rightly that her services wouldn't be missed in the kitchen for the next few minutes and had run out the back way to talk with Neil. As she approached him, he came down the path to meet her.

"I was so afraid you wouldn't come!" he said. Trixie thought he sounded like a little boy.

"I *said* I would, didn't I?" she answered with a hint of a smile. "But I only have a few minutes, so tell me what you have on your mind."

"Well, I guess you know what I was after when I came to Cliveden," he began, kicking the gravel in the path with the toe of his shoe.

"I can guess," Trixie answered, "but I can't figure out how you got here from Croton so fast."

"Oh, that was easy," he explained. "Almost too easy to be true. The day after Miss Julie told me about the necklace, I went down to the farm to help with the horses, and there was this van waiting to pick up one of the mares to take to Virginia."

"And you managed to hitch a ride to Cliveden?" Trixie asked.

"Not all the way, but almost," Neil said, "and when I got here, I heard about Jenkins and his stable being at Rosewood, and I got me a job."

"Yes, yes! Go on," Trixie urged impatiently.

"Well, at first Jenkins seemed like an okay guy, and I told him what I'd heard about the lost necklace, thinking he could help me and we could split the loot," Neil continued. "Right after that, he began to treat me mean and beat me. He beat the horses, too, and that got to me! I can take care of myself, but I don't like to see no animals hurt." He paused briefly, shaking his head, before he went on.

"Then, that day in the cemetery— I guess you wonder why I broke in on you that way," he said.

"Well, it *was* rather unexpected," Trixie said, trying to repress a chuckle. "What *was* your idea?"

"You see, my old man—I mean, my father's a

cripple, like Mr. Carver, always in a wheelchair. Got his legs smashed in a machine when I was a kid." Neil, hands thrust deep in his pockets, his head low, was having trouble continuing, but Trixie didn't hurry him. After a pause he looked up at her and went on. "He's a great guy. He never complains, and he makes all kinds of things with his hands, but it was always hard times for my mother and my two sisters and me. That's why I quit school and scrammed out of there. School wasn't really *that* bad, but I couldn't go on sitting down to supper every night and seeing Mom and Pop going without so us kids would have enough. I *had* to do something!"

"I'll admit that's enough to make anyone want to do something drastic," Trixie replied sympathetically, "but I still don't see what it has to do with your attack on us yesterday."

"It's on account of Mr. Carver, really," Neil continued. "I saw him the first day, when I was out exercising one of the horses. He was sitting in his wheelchair out in the garden, drawing or painting or something, and I . . . well . . . I just felt awful sorry for him. I didn't want anyone to do anything to hurt him. See?"

"Yes," Trixie said slowly. "I see. As a matter of fact, I sort of half suspected something like that, but why are you telling me all this?"

"Because now I know you don't mean no harm to him, and I want to get away from Jenkins and never have to see him again!"

"Okay," Trixie said gently, placing her hand on his arm. "I believe you. I can't talk to you any more right now, but you meet us down the road when we leave this afternoon, and we'll try to figure out what's the best thing for you to do."

Neil's thanks were still ringing in her ears as she went back to the kitchen.

"Where have *you* been?" Honey and Di demanded as she came in. "You're just in time to see the dishes all washed and put away."

"I'm sorry I couldn't help clean up," Trixie said, "but, believe it or not, I've been having a very interesting conversation with Neil."

"Neil!" they cried in disbelief. "Where did you find Neil?"

"He found me!" Trixie laughed. "I'll tell you all about it in a minute. Where are the boys?"

"Brian's gone with the doctor, I guess," Di said, "and Mart and Jim are in the study."

"Let's go in there," Trixie suggested. "They'll want to hear about Neil, too."

They found Mart and Jim trying to figure out a way to fix Mr. Carver's wheelchair.

"Don't worry about that right now," Trixie said. "I've got news for all of you." She proceeded to tell them of her encounter with Neil.

"Well, what do you know!" Mart cried when she had finished. "Another coup for the head of the Belden Detective Agency. Take a bow, Trixie the Shamus!"

"Oh, cut it out, Mart," Trixie snapped. "This isn't the time for any of your brilliant comments. Neil is in trouble and needs help badly. We've got to think of something to do."

"I somehow don't think Neil's going to be a problem for long," Jim commented. "Now that he realizes he was on the wrong track, he has half the battle won. A good job and a little guidance are what he needs now."

"We'll work out something," Trixie said, "once we put our minds to it, but right now we've got to think about the cellar. I wish I'd thought to ask Mr. Carver how to get down there."

"Oh, he told us before he left," Mart said. "The door's in the front hall."

"Let's get going, then," Trixie said eagerly, heading for the front of the house.

"That one under the stairs must be it," Jim conjectured, pointing to a door fastened with a big brass lock.

Trixie pushed back the bolt, switched on the light inside, and started down the steps.

"I'd say that bulb must have been one of Mr. Edison's originals," Mart observed as he looked over Trixie's shoulder at the one small bulb casting a dim glow down the stairs. "Why didn't we bring flashlights?"

When Trixie got almost to the bottom of the stairs, she let out a loud *eeeek* and turned and grabbed Jim, who was right behind her.

"What's the matter, Trixie? The ghost?" he asked with a chuckle.

"I don't know what it was!" Trixie answered. "Something brushed my forehead!"

Jim pushed ahead of her, holding his hand in front of his face. Almost immediately another light came on, and Trixie, realizing that what she had felt was only a pull cord, laughed with relief.

"You and your ghosts!" Mart scoffed. "What next?"

"Well, I notice you brought up the rear very bravely," Trixie taunted.

"Only my natural good manners," Mart countered. "Women and children first, you know."

As the Bob-Whites edged their way farther into the shadows of the cellar, which still was not lighted well enough to be clearly visible, Trixie suddenly snapped her fingers.

"I'll bet there's an outside hatch," she said. "If we can find it and open it up, it would give us more light."

"I'll go and see," Mart volunteered, eager to make up for the ribbing he had given his sister.

It wasn't long before the Bob-Whites heard a rapping and saw a stream of light appear as Mart opened the double doors of the wide outside entrance to the basement.

"That's more like it," Di exclaimed with a shiver. "Isn't it funny how our imaginations work overtime in the dark? I could swear I heard a tapping sound a minute ago, but it's gone now."

"Well," Honey said plaintively, "I certainly hope it wasn't the ghost!"

"Nonsense," Jim answered, trying to be reassuring. "There isn't any such thing."

The walls of the cellar were built of stone, like the foundations they had seen at Rosewood Hall, and there were the same massive supporting pillars. The floor was dirt, but so hard-packed that it looked like concrete. It was quite evident that the room had been cleaned out fairly recently. Only a few large stone crocks remained, along with an old wooden cabinet holding an assortment of bottles and jars.

"Well, someone has gone over this place with a fine-tooth comb," Trixie said in an exasperated tone when they had finished a painstaking examination of the cellar. "There aren't even any cobwebs left!"

She stood in the middle of the chamber, hands on hips and elbows akimbo, looking around to be sure they hadn't overlooked anything.

"There's just one more thing we'd better do," she said slowly. "Let's move that cabinet and see what's behind it. It's the only part of the wall we haven't examined."

"And it's on the side nearest Rosewood Hall," Jim observed, starting to take the contents from the shelves and placing them on the floor.

When the boys had moved the heavy oak case a few feet away from the wall, Trixie peered behind it.

"Gleeps!" she exclaimed. "I was right! This part of

the wall isn't stone at all. It's brick! And I'll bet the secret passage is behind it!"

"But why would anyone want to close up the entrance?" Honey asked.

"And *when* was it done?" Jim wondered. "This looks like a fairly recent job to me."

Mart tapped the bricks with his knuckles, holding his ear close to the wall to see if it sounded hollow.

"Can't tell a thing," he said despondently. "Do you think we should knock a hole in it?" .

"Oh, of course not!" Trixie cried. "At least not until we've asked Mr. Carver or—Jeepers! I'd forgotten all about Miss Bates! Maybe she'd know something about it. I wonder if Mr. Carver phoned her."

Just as she asked the question, the Bob-Whites heard the beep-beep of the station wagon horn. They nearly fell over each other as they raced up the hatchway steps to the driveway.

Two Feet of Space • 13

Dr. Brandon and Brian were lifting Mr. Carver out of the station wagon as the girls, Jim, and Mart came up the driveway. Trixie sensed by the sound of their laughter that the doctor's further examination had confirmed his earlier belief that Mr. Carver hadn't been seriously injured.

"Come and see my new wheelchair," he called out when he saw the Bob-Whites. "It has everything except a motor."

"I'll supply the horsepower," Jim volunteered, starting to push the chair. "Wow! This makes your old chair look like a Model T Ford!"

"And it even folds up so it can be carried in a small car," Brian said.

"It's one I keep in the office for just such emergencies," Dr. Brandon explained, "and Edgar is welcome to use it as long as he needs it."

Everyone, feeling a sense of relief that Mr. Carver was all right, chattered gaily on their way to the house.

Trixie, of course, was dying to ask Mr. Carver about the bricked-up section they had found in the cellar, but she waited until he had been made comfortable on the sofa in the study. Dr. Brandon put some pills on a nearby table before leaving and suggested that the injured man take it easy for a day or so.

"This thing has been quite a shock, but fortunately there has been no real damage. Knowing my friend's strong constitution *and* stubborn disposition, I'd say he'll be himself in no time."

Mr. Carver must have been reading Trixie's thoughts, for he had no sooner said good-bye to the doctor than he turned to her.

"Now, Trixie," he said, "give me a progress report. What did you find while I was away?"

"Well, there isn't anything in the cellar, really, to give us any leads," Trixie began, "except one part of the wall. It's built of brick instead of stone and looks a lot newer than the rest of the foundation. Do you know anything about it?"

"You're right," Mr. Carver said. "It is new construction. It was put in only a year ago, when that part of the wall started to crumble. I don't know why they used bricks instead of stone, unless they found them easier to work with."

"And there wasn't anything on the other side?"

Mart asked. "Are you sure of that?"

"Nothing but good old Virginia soil, I'm afraid," Mr. Carver said with a laugh.

"Another dead end!" Trixie moaned, dropping into a chair.

"What about Miss Bates?" Di asked, looking from Trixie to Edgar Carver. "Didn't you think she might help us?"

"Oh, I'd completely forgotten dear Miss Bates," he said, glancing at his watch. "She said she'd drop by around three, and it's almost that now."

"Well, that gives us one more chance," Trixie said, forcing a smile. She strolled over to the French doors. Looking out, she saw a woman, holding on to a floppy straw hat with one hand and carrying a basket of flowers with the other, making her way toward the terrace.

"Here comes someone now," Trixie called out, turning to Mr. Carver. "Do you suppose it's Miss Bates?"

"If she has a load of flowers, it's sure to be." Mr. Carver smiled. "She almost never comes without bringing something from her own garden to brighten up Green Trees."

Miss Bates breezed into the room like a ship under full sail. She plunked the huge basket of flowers down on the floor, then stepped back to take a long look at Edgar Carver, seemingly unaware of the others in the room.

"Heavens to Betsy!" she exclaimed, bending over him to take a closer look at the bandage through her thick glasses. "Whatever in the world happened to you?"

"Oh, just a little accident," he reassured her. "I fell out of my chair and cut my forehead this morning, but Alex says it's nothing to worry about."

"Pooh! That's a man's opinion," Miss Bates pronounced firmly, settling her ample frame and voluminous skirts in the chair she had drawn up near the couch. "What *you* need is some calf's-foot jelly and custard to build up your strength and a good poultice of bread and milk to draw out the poison from that wound."

Edgar Carver smiled indulgently at his friend, as though accustomed to her sometimes wild theories. He then beckoned to the Bob-Whites, who had been watching this little scene from a distance.

"I do declare," Miss Bates chirped, drawing off a pair of long white lace gloves, "it's good to have young people in the house—that is, if they don't go around breaking things and disturbing you with a lot of noise. Now, you take those wild nieces of mine—"

"No, Carolyn," Mr. Carver broke in with a chuckle, "we don't want to take your nieces! These friends of mine are not in the least obstreperous. As a matter of fact, they are here because of a real interest in Green Trees. Trixie found a letter—up north, where she lives—that leads us to believe there is, or was, a secret passage between Green Trees and Rosewood Hall, and we hope you may be able to shed some light on it. That's why I asked you to bring over the floor plans that were used in the remodeling."

"Well, of all things!" Miss Bates said. She seemed unable to say anything without prefacing her remarks with an exclamation. "It doesn't seem possible. Not after all the work we've done around here. Nothing we ever found suggested such a thing. Are you sure?" She turned a dubious eye on Trixie for affirmation.

"No," admitted Trixie hesitantly, "we can't be sure, of course, but we thought we'd explore the possibilities, as long as we were down here and Mr. Carver was willing for us to look around."

Mr. Carver then told Miss Bates of Mr. Lynch's interest in old estates and of his trip to Williamsburg.

"And that's how Trixie and her friends happened to come to Green Trees," Mr. Carver told her.

"You don't say!" Miss Bates exclaimed. "Why, I was up to some of those meetings in Williamsburg myself. I thought I might get some tips from some of the other members, you know."

"I guess you could give *them* some tips," Edgar Carver said warmly. "I don't know anyone who knows more about Colonial houses than Miss Carolyn here," he told the Bob-Whites.

"Oh, Edgar, how you do run on!" the ample lady said, her pink cheeks growing several shades pinker.

She's right out of Colonial America herself, Trixie thought as she watched and listened to this unusual woman. Mr. Carver's compliment seemed to have left Miss Bates speechless, for the moment at least, so Trixie asked, "Do you think it might help if we looked at the plans Mr. Carver said you had drawn up?"

"Why, of course, child," she replied, "but *I* didn't draw them up. One of the local contractors who did a lot of the reconstruction made the plans."

She took up the basket and, summoning Honey and Di to her, thrust the mountain of blooms into their hands and suggested they put them in water. "You two look as though you might be used to caring for flowers," she said as she waved them away and started to paw through a pile of papers in the bottom of the basket. Honey fled to the kitchen, followed by Di. Both were having difficulty suppressing their laughter.

"And *you* look like the one with a real head on your shoulders," she added, handing Trixie a sheaf of papers. Miss Bates completely ignored the boys, who wisely stayed in the background for the time being.

Trixie took the plans over to the desk and spread them out. The first one showed the cellar, indicating the location of the new brickwork. There seemed to be nothing more of any significance on that page. The next showed part of the first floor: the drawing room, dining room, music salon, and solarium. Trixie traced the outlines of the rooms with a finger, picturing each one in her mind's eye. Then, noticing that Miss Bates was deep in conversation with Mr. Carver, she motioned for Jim, Mart, and Brian to come over and look at the plans. They were soon joined by Honey and Di, who had disposed of the floral offering by plunging the flowers into a pail of water in the kitchen, to be arranged later.

"Do you see anything helpful?" Di asked, bending over Trixie's shoulder. "Blueprints are a complete puzzle to me."

"Well, *this* one puzzles *me*," Trixie conceded. "See here, between the music room and the solarium? There are two lines instead of one. I don't remember anything between those two rooms."

"Could it be closet space?" Jim asked, taking a closer look at the drawing.

"Possibly," Trixie said, chewing the end of her finger, "but there's no door showing here, and I don't remember seeing one, either, do you?"

"Maybe it's in the hall," Brian suggested. "I'll go take a look."

He returned almost immediately to say there was no door, only a space of about two feet between the music room partition and the solarium.

"That's just what it shows here," Trixie whispered. "Wait, I'll go ask Miss Bates."

"Didn't I tell you, Edgar, this one's the one with the brains?" Miss Bates challenged him after Trixie had pointed out the discrepancy on the blueprint.

"But, Carolyn, my dear, I never *said* Trixie was anything but brilliant, did I?" Mr. Carver said with a wink at the Bob-Whites.

"No, no, no," Miss Bates said impatiently. "I didn't mean that at all. I only meant Trixie put her finger right on something that's been puzzling all of us who had anything to do with this house. The outside

measurements just don't jibe with the inside, and
I've checked them three times with my own tape
measure!"

"You mean there's this little triangular space left
over, like a gusset in a sleeve?" Honey said, pointing
to the area in question.

"Exactly," Miss Bates replied, flipping shut the
Japanese fan with which she had been cooling herself since her arrival and tapping it briskly on the
arm of the chair. "Probably the mistake of the original
builder. A man, I'm sure. But I mean to find out as
soon as we start on the music room."

"And when will that be?" Trixie asked anxiously.

"In the fall, probably," Miss Bates answered. "As
soon as the tourist season is over. I doubt if we'll find
anything of interest, but I'll write you if we do."

"Then you don't think it has anything to do with
the secret passage?" Trixie asked, her face clouded.

"One chance in a million," Miss Bates replied, settling her hat more firmly on her head and jabbing an
enormous hat pin through it. "In all my experience,
I've never seen a three-cornered room, with no door
and no window, only two feet at its widest point.
Have you? It was a plain mistake, I'll wager, and if
not, I'll eat this hat, complete with all the cabbage
roses on it!"

She got up and gave Edgar Carver's hand a squeeze,
pronouncing him to be the only man in Christendom
who had any sense, although there were times when
she despaired even of him. Then, waving in the

general direction of the Bob-Whites, she was off.

Everyone seemed a little breathless after her departure, and, although there were seven people present, the room appeared strangely empty.

"I guess I should have warned you that Carolyn is something of a character," Mr. Carver said. "I've known her for years, and she never seems to run out of steam."

"She *does* have a lot of energy," Trixie commented, "and she also seems to have very positive ideas."

"Well, when you get to know her as well as I do, you'll find out that when she is the most vehement about something, she may be covering up a secret reservation," Mr. Carver replied.

"You mean she thinks there's more to the secret passage than she cares to admit?" Trixie asked.

"Just that," he answered. "She hates to think she didn't discover it for herself, but you'll find that if *you* locate it, she'll be the first to give you credit. You wait and see. She'll be back tomorrow, with her custard and poultices, to see what you've found."

"Jeepers, Mr. Carver," Trixie said, "I hate to think of Miss Bates eating that enormous hat and all those roses, but I have a feeling she's going to have to!"

"Well, dressed up with a little mayonnaise, it might not be so bad," Mart quipped.

Trixie was only half listening. She walked over to the corner of the study nearest the controversial partition and began carefully looking over the bookshelves which lined that side of the room. Then,

leaving the other Bob-Whites in a discussion with
Mr. Carver, she slipped out into the hall and into
the music room. She took a long time going over the
beautiful paneling on the walls, frequently tapping
her fingers on the wood or gently pushing against
the wall with her shoulder. Having circled the room,
she returned to that part of the wall that backed
against the study and reexamined it with special
care, even getting down on her knees to have a good
look at the baseboard. As she felt along it, she noticed a depression under one of the moldings.

"It's just what I suspected," she said to herself.
"It's almost as though I *knew* what I'd find. Now if
my hunch only continues to work!"

She felt a shiver of excitement run up her spine.
Placing her fingers in the little hollowed-out space,
she pushed up, as though opening a window, and
after several jerks, she felt the panel begin to slide.
She lifted it as far as it would go, revealing a space
about half the height of the room. She took a fleeting
glance into the dark opening, then dashed back to
the study.

"I've found it!" she cried. "Come here! Quick!"

She grabbed Honey by the hand and, followed by
the other Bob-Whites, ran back to the music room to
show them her discovery. They took turns looking
into the murky space, while Trixie hurried back to
tell Mr. Carver more about it. She found him swing-
ing himself into his wheelchair, his face bright with
expectation.

"Oh, Mr. Carver, you shouldn't be moving around like this!" Trixie cried. "I'll tell you everything!"

"No, my dear," he replied. "This I must see for myself."

As they started toward the door, they met Jim coming to ask if there was a flashlight in the house.

"It's so dark in that little cubbyhole, we can't make out a thing," he said, "except that it doesn't seem to have a floor."

"No floor!" Trixie exclaimed. "What do you mean?"

"There's a flashlight here in the drawer," Mr. Carver said, steering his chair near enough to reach it. "This may be the beginning of the end of the mystery."

The Bob-Whites stood back to let Trixie have the first real look inside the opening. She felt the familiar pounding in her heart as she bent down and shot a beam of light into the blackness.

"What do you see, Trix?"

"Don't keep us in the dark!"

"Let us look!"

The Bob-Whites were all talking at once, now that the first excitement of discovery was over.

Trixie stood up, her face glowing. "Jim's right," she said. "There isn't a floor, but there *is* a narrow circular stairway leading down to the cellar!"

"To the cellar!" Mart exclaimed. "Then how come we didn't see it when we were down there?"

"Jeepers! I don't know!" Trixie said in bewilderment. "Maybe the staircase doesn't lead to the cellar at all! Wait a minute, and I'll go down and see where it goes."

She stepped gingerly into the narrow opening, and, holding the flashlight in front of her, she disappeared into the darkness below.

A Narrow Escape · 14

ARE YOU ALL RIGHT, Trixie?" Jim called to her. "Do you want me to come down there, too?" His voice sounded strangely hollow in the confined space.

Almost like an echo Trixie answered, "I'm all right, Jim. No, don't come down. There's barely enough room for me."

"Are you at the bottom yet?" Mart called, leaning over Jim's shoulder. They could not see Trixie because of the curve in the staircase, but the ghostly glow of her light was reflected up to them.

"No, not yet." Her voice now sounded even farther away. "It's funny. I should be near the cellar by now, but the stairs seem to keep right on going. Don't worry. I'm all right. I'm just getting a little out of breath."

"What did she say?" Mr. Carver inquired, leaning expectantly forward in his chair.

"She said she was getting short of breath," Jim answered.

At this Brian jumped up, a worried look coming over his face, and, pushing the others away from the entrance to the stairwell, yelled down to Trixie.

"Don't go a step farther, Trixie. Turn around and come right back! The air in there is probably dead. You hear me?"

"Yes, Brian," Trixie replied, her voice somewhat weaker than before. "I'm coming. It is—pretty stuffy—down here." Her words came slowly, too slowly to satisfy Jim, who turned to Brian.

"I'm going in there! I think she needs help!"

As Jim descended, there was complete silence in the room. Then, after what seemed like an eternity, he reappeared, and right behind him came Trixie, looking paler than any of the Bob-Whites remembered ever seeing her. She dropped into a chair, stretched out her legs, and threw back her head. Brian was at her side immediately.

"Put your head down between your knees, Trix," he ordered. "Mart, open the window. She's faint. Grab hold of the chair, Jim, and we'll carry her over to where she can get some fresh air."

It wasn't long before the color began to come back to Trixie's cheeks, and a slow smile spread over her face.

"Gleeps!" she said, lifting her head. "Another minute of that foul air, and I would have been a goner. If I hadn't had Jim's foot to grab on to, I don't think I could have made it back."

"Well, I don't think we'd better let you try any more descents today," Mr. Carver said, a look of relief flooding over his face as he saw Trixie revive. "I'll tell you what I suggest. I'll hook up an electric fan tonight and leave this window open, so that by tomorrow there should be some air circulating down there."

"Could you see any opening at the bottom?" Mart asked Trixie.

"I didn't *get* to the bottom," she answered impatiently. "That's what puzzles me. I'm sure I went down to the cellar level, because I counted the steps, and I was on the twentieth one when Brian called to me to come back."

"Let's not worry about that right now," Mr. Carver said, giving her arm a pat. "I think, my dear, a good night's sleep is what we all need. We've had more than our share of excitement today." Then, turning to Jim, he said, "Get her back to Williamsburg, Jim, and see that she takes it easy this evening."

"That's a difficult order." Jim laughed. "Trixie isn't one to take it easy very often, but I'll try."

"That's a splendid idea, Mr. Carver," Honey said. "I guess we could all stand a quiet evening for a change, and we still have one more day, before we leave for home, to see what's at the bottom of the stairs."

"That's not much time," Trixie sighed, "but with luck, we may solve the mystery tomorrow, so keep your fingers crossed, all of you!"

It wasn't until the Bob-Whites were settled in the station wagon and turning out of the drive that Trixie, suddenly snapping her fingers, remembered Neil.

"We've got to talk with him, if he's still waiting for us," she said emphatically.

"Oh, Trixie, can't you put him off until tomorrow?" Honey pleaded. "You must be dead tired. I know *I* am, and I haven't been through what you have today."

"No," Trixie answered in the same positive tone. "If we don't talk to him now, when he's ready for help, he may get discouraged and fall into worse trouble than before."

"Trixie's right," Jim said. "We don't have to take much time—just assure him that we're ready to help and maybe offer some suggestions."

They had gone past Rosewood Hall and were beginning to wonder if perhaps Neil had lost patience and decided not to wait for them, when Trixie spotted him. He was sitting under a tree by the side of the road.

"Hi, Neil," she called out as Jim brought the car to a stop.

Neil got to his feet but seemed hesitant about coming closer until Trixie said reassuringly, "Come on over and meet the rest of my friends."

He then walked slowly toward them, twisting his cap in his hands and looking almost shyly from one to the other. Honey remarked later that she wouldn't have known he was the same brash boy she had met at Miss Julie's.

"Jim, here, I think you've met before," Trixie said with the hint of a laugh.

"Yes, we met under rather unusual circumstances the other day," Jim said, smiling warmly, "but let's forget about that."

At this sign of friendship from Jim, Neil began to be more at ease and acknowledged each introduction with a "Pleased to meet you" and a bob of his head.

"Hop in, if you can find room, and we'll give you a lift," Trixie said. "We're awfully late, so we'll have to talk on the way."

"That's all right with me," Neil answered. "I'm not going anywhere special."

"Not to Texas?" Trixie asked this with the trace of a smile as Neil got into the front seat with Jim and her.

"Huh-uh!" Neil said emphatically. "That was just a wild dream. I'm always having wild dreams, like that necklace business."

"Trixie tells us you quit Jenkins," Brian said. "Got any plans now, wild or not?" His tone was so genial that they could almost see Neil's confidence returning to him.

"Well," he began slowly, "I want to get a job. I still like to work with horses, and I want to finish up high school, too, but I guess I can't do both."

"How much longer do you have to go?" Mart asked.

"Only a year," Neil replied. "I'd have graduated

last June if I hadn't up and quit."

Di hadn't said anything during this conversation, but as Neil finished, she leaned forward from the backseat.

"You know," she said, "I think Daddy might be able to suggest something. He's wonderful about helping people if he thinks they really want to help themselves."

"Oh, I do!" Neil said. "Honestly, I do. All I want is a chance!"

"Well, you come back with us to Williamsburg, and I'll see when he can talk with you," Di said. "You'll like Daddy. He had a hard time when he was your age, too, so he'll understand," she added softly.

"What's Jenkins up to these days?" Trixie asked, trying to make her voice sound casual.

"Oh, he keeps digging around in the ruins of Rose-wood Hall," Neil said. "He's sure the emeralds are there somewhere. He even talks about a secret passage. What a crazy idea!"

Hmmm! Trixie thought to herself. *Apparently Jenkins didn't tell Neil about the message in the locket, or he wouldn't think the idea so crazy.* Then, aloud, she asked, "Do *you* still think they're there?"

"I don't know, and, frankly, I don't care. They've got me in enough hot water already. I just hope *you* find 'em before *he* does!"

"So do we!" Trixie said earnestly. "But I might as well be frank with you. So far we've had no luck."

Mr. and Mrs. Lynch were walking up and down in

front of the cottage as they drove up. It was obvious, from the looks on their faces, that they were worried about the Bob-Whites getting back so much later than usual, but Di hurried to set their minds at ease. Then their anxiety gave way to curiosity when they saw Neil in the car.

"This is our friend Neil," Di said, "and he'd like to talk to you, Daddy, if you have a few minutes."

Mr. Lynch gave Di and Neil an appraising look and then said, "Suppose we go inside, where we'll have some privacy, and you can tell me what's on your mind."

"I'd like to have Di and Trixie come with me, if you don't mind," Neil said. "This was sort of their idea, and I'd feel better if they were along." His face reddened as he said this, but Mr. Lynch was quick to reassure him.

"Of course, of course," he said. "You others go for a swim while we have a little chat, and then we'll meet in time for dinner." Putting his arm around Neil's shoulders, he went into the cottage, followed by Trixie and Di.

Trixie realized that the time had come to tell Mr. Lynch about the letter she had found in the attic at Crabapple Farm and the circumstances of her first meeting with Neil. He listened attentively to her story, smiling occasionally when Trixie's enthusiasm made her get ahead of herself and forced her to backtrack in her account of what had happened.

"And did you all plan to meet Neil down here and

hunt for the treasure?" he asked when Trixie had finished.

"No, sir," Neil spoke for the first time. "I came down on my own hook." Then he went on to tell about his encounter with Jenkins and his change of heart about going on with the search.

"So you see, Daddy," Di broke in, "we hoped you'd have some suggestion about where Neil might get work or something."

"Then I take it no one has found the necklace." Mr. Lynch looked from one to the other.

"No," Trixie answered. "That is, *we* haven't—and so far as we know, Jenkins hasn't, either."

"Well, that's something I'll have to leave up to you, I guess. Treasure hunts are a little out of my line." He smiled indulgently at the two girls. "But Neil's problem is something I may be able to do something about."

"Oh, I knew you would, Daddy!" Di said fervently. "What do you plan?"

"Well, that's a good question, dear," her father replied. "Several things suggest themselves to me, but it will take a little time to decide what's best for this young man. Suppose you come back tomorrow about this time, and we'll talk again."

"That'll be great, Mr. Lynch!" Neil said. "You can count on me from now on!"

"I'm sure I can," Di's father answered, extending his hand to Neil. "And by the way, my boy, how about a small loan to take care of your needs for the next day or so? You'd be welcome to it."

"No, thank you," Neil said proudly. "I still have some of my pay. I'll make out just fine!" Then turning a warm smile on Trixie and Di, he said, "Be seeing you," and he was gone.

"Well, this trip has turned out to be quite a little adventure." Mr. Lynch laughed. "Of course, we don't really know anything about this Neil, but he impresses me as being sincere, and I'm ready to give him a chance."

"You're the greatest!" Di said, giving her father an affectionate kiss. "Now we'd better go and get dressed for dinner. I'm starved. Come on, Trix."

Trixie was dead tired, but a hot shower and fresh clothes did much to revive her. By the time they all met for dinner, she had regained most of her natural bounce. After everyone had ordered, Mr. Lynch leaned back in his chair.

"Trixie," he said, "I didn't want to show too much curiosity about this necklace while I was talking to Neil a while ago, but now I would like to ask you, in all seriousness, if you really believe there's a secret passage, let alone an emerald necklace."

"I know it's hard to believe, Mr. Lynch," Trixie answered soberly. "I guess that's why we didn't tell you all the details the other day when you finally suspected that we were on the trail of a mystery. Until today, there were times when I was ready to give up."

"What happened today?" Mrs. Lynch asked

eagerly. "Did you find any clues?"

"You sound just like a Bob-White, Mummy," Di said with a laugh. "We're always asking Trixie if she's uncovered any more clues. Go on, tell what you found in the music room, Trixie."

"Well, I just happened to hit on a secret staircase," Trixie said, "a circular one going down to the cellar and maybe beyond."

"I love the way she says she 'just happened' to hit on it," Jim chuckled. "Trixie figured the whole thing out after she'd seen the blueprints, with no help from any of us."

Trixie took a sip of water and hoped that no one noticed the color that she could feel mounting in her cheeks. Honey, realizing how embarrassed Trixie was, began to elaborate on the discovery so attention would be drawn away from her friend for a few minutes. By the time she had finished, dinner was served, and they became so engrossed in the delicious Southern fried chicken, corn fritters, and buttery mashed potatoes that conversation lagged, and Mr. Lynch seemed in no hurry to press the Bob-Whites for more details. Then, after they had managed to make away with an assortment of luscious sundaes, he asked, very casually, if they were planning to pursue their exploration of the secret staircase the next day.

"Oh, of course!" Trixie cried. "It's our last chance. It's tomorrow or never—at least, never for us." She wondered why Mr. Lynch smiled as she said this. It was almost as though he had a secret he wasn't willing to share just yet.

"I must try to get out to Green Trees before we go home," he said. "I've heard a lot about it and what a wonderful job of restoration they're doing. Maybe I can make it tomorrow afternoon."

"Oh, I'd love to have you see it!" Trixie replied with enthusiasm.

"And you really should meet Mr. Carver," Di added. "He's a marvelous person. You and Mummy would like him, I know."

Just as they were going into the cottage after dinner, the phone rang. Mrs. Lynch answered it, then called Trixie. "It's for you, dear," she said, handing the receiver over.

A puzzled look came over Trixie's face.

Maybe it's Neil, she thought. *I can't imagine who else would be calling me.*

It was apparent immediately that what was being said on the other end of the wire came as a shock, for Trixie slumped into the chair near the telephone, a look of bewilderment coming over her face.

"He *has?*" the others heard her say. "Where? When?"

After listening for a moment longer, she ended the conversation.

"Yes, we'll be out in the morning," she said. "Around ten? Yes. I'll try not to worry. Thanks, Mr. Carver."

She slowly replaced the receiver in its cradle. Then,

looking up, her face a picture of despair, she said, "I guess you heard. It was Mr. Carver. Jenkins has just phoned to tell him he's found the necklace!"

"Oh, no!" Honey cried. "I can't believe it."

"He's coming over with it in the morning, and Mr. Carver wanted us to be there," Trixie added.

"Did Mr. Carver say what kind of deal Jenkins wants to make?" Mr. Lynch asked. "From what you tell me about the fellow, I'm sure he has something up his sleeve."

"No," Trixie replied. "He just said Jenkins was coming and wanted to talk with him." She obviously was making a valiant effort to keep the tears back.

"Well, I hate to have you go out there alone and run the risk of getting into any kind of trouble," Mr. Lynch said. "But with the boys along, I'm sure you'll be able to cope with Jenkins. I'd go with you, but I have an important engagement in the morning. However, I'll come out right after I've finished."

"Well, knowing how Jenkins acted when Lizzie James threatened him, I don't think we have anything to worry about," Trixie assured him. "But who knows what he plans to do with the emeralds?"

Although the Bob-Whites retired early, hoping that sleep would blot out the awful disappointment they all felt, it was not easy for any of them to put it out of their minds. Trixie's brain was in a turmoil. Even though she kept telling herself that she should be glad, for Mr. Carver's sake, that the jewels had been found, she couldn't mask the despair she felt.

Miss Bates Is Surprised • 15

THE BOB-WHITES were in just as depressed a mood the next morning as they had been the night before. All the excitement of the vacation trip seemed to have evaporated. After they had ridden toward Green Trees for some time in silence, Trixie said, "You know, I wouldn't have cared half so much if anybody else had found the emeralds—Miss Bates or Mr. Carver or even Neil—but *Jenkins!* It makes me boil just to think of it!"

"I can't wait to hear what he has to say," Honey said, "and how he found them."

"Well, I still can't believe it's true," Trixie mused. "He probably stumbled across the entrance to the passage where some of the masonry had caved in."

"I wonder if he's at Green Trees yet," Mart speculated. "Now that he has the necklace, I don't suppose Mr. Carver is in any more danger from him."

"It's funny"—Trixie frowned—"but I still don't know if Jenkins actually stole the message from the locket that day or even if Mr. Carver remembers if he did."

"It's possible he could have had a spell of amnesia from that blow on his head," Brian said.

"You mean he actually may not remember what went on before he fell out of his chair?" Di asked.

"That sort of thing sometimes happens," Brian replied.

"Do they ever remember later on?" Honey pursued.

"Sometimes yes, sometimes no," Brian said. "Actually, very little is known about how the brain stores up impressions or what really causes temporary lapses of memory."

"Maybe we'll find out more about it when we see Mr. Carver and Jenkins this morning," Trixie said.

As they were approaching the house, they saw Jenkins walking hastily across the lawn toward the terrace. They waited long enough for him to go inside before putting in an appearance themselves. Mr. Carver was at the door when they arrived. He welcomed them cordially and asked them to come in and meet his neighbor.

It was evident that Jenkins hadn't expected the Bob-Whites to be there, for when he saw them, the crooked smile disappeared from his face, and his jaw dropped in disbelief. It took him several seconds to regain enough composure to respond as Mr. Carver introduced the Bob-Whites by their first names.

Following Trixie's cue, none of them let on they

had ever seen Jenkins before. This seemed to confuse the man further, and he twisted uncomfortably in his chair. When Mr. Carver asked him coldly to state his business, he looked from one to the other, as if uncertain of the wisdom of speaking with the young people present.

"Maybe I ought to come back later," Jenkins said in a whining voice. "Neil, the boy, said you had an accident you don't remember. . . ."

As he said this, it seemed to Trixie that he was searching, feeling Mr. Carver out to see if he remembered anything about the fall he had taken. Trixie glanced at the Bob-Whites. Each of them, she knew, realized that Jenkins was projecting a lie—that he knew very well what had happened to Edgar Carver.

"Never mind the sympathy, Jenkins," Mr. Carver said with a wave of his hand. "The accident is my affair; I don't even remember what happened. These young people are all friends of mine, so you go right ahead and state your business."

Trixie saw the look of relief in Jenkins's face as he heard Mr. Carver confess that he remembered nothing of the accident. He then fumbled in the pocket of his worn tweed riding coat and drew out a small tin box. He didn't open it but got up and, walking over to Mr. Carver, handed it to him.

"This is the box I found at Rosewood Hall," he said gruffly. "I figured, since your family and the folks that used to live at Rosewood were pretty close, you might be interested in it."

Mr. Carver opened the box and gazed for a long time at the contents. Then he handed it to Trixie.

"Mr. Jenkins has apparently come across something of considerable value, Trixie. He found this in the ruins of Rosewood Hall," he said sadly. "They are truly beautiful gems, aren't they?"

Trixie took the little box and forced herself to look inside. She couldn't keep the tears from her eyes.

"Why, yes," she said with some hesitation, "it's a lovely necklace. I've never seen anything quite like it."

She held it up for Di and Honey to see, giving them a covert wink, and they, too, said it was beautiful. Then she closed the box and turned her attention to the cover. Although it was quite rusty, it still showed signs of printing on the top. No one seemed to notice Trixie's absorption in it. They were too busy listening to Jenkins, who, now that the necklace had been so much admired, was becoming more expansive by the minute.

"The young lady's right," he said. "It's a rare piece and worth a lot of money. I could have sold it to a dealer friend of mine, but I've got a sentimental streak in me, and I figured Mr. Carver, here, would like it."

"You mean—" Mr. Carver started to say.

"I mean I'm willing to let you have it for a fraction of what the thing is really worth," Jenkins said, a cunning smile on his face. "It's yours for four hundred dollars, and you can't say that's not giving it away. You'll never get a bigger bargain."

Trixie didn't bat an eye as she gave the box back to Mr. Carver. She prayed silently that he wouldn't make a deal right then and there. She desperately wanted time. There were several things she *had* to know. There were no tears in her eyes now, nor had there been from the moment she had taken a good look at the contents of the little tin box.

"Four hundred dollars!" Mr. Carver said slowly, again opening the box and gazing at the necklace. "I'm afraid it will take some time to raise such a large amount of money. Could you give me a day or so to see what arrangements I can make?"

"Yes, yes," Jenkins said, his manner becoming more and more affable as he saw the possibility of his offer being accepted. "Take your time. I don't want to put no pressure on you. What say if I come back tomorrow afternoon?"

"Well, that doesn't give me much time," Mr. Carver said, his voice uncommonly low, "but I'll see what I can do."

This arrangement being apparently satisfactory to Jenkins, he seemed eager for the interview to be over. After pocketing the box and giving a perfunctory nod in the general direction of the Bob-Whites, he went away.

Mr. Carver sat slowly stroking his forehead, until Trixie came over and plopped down on the floor in front of him.

"Do you *really* believe what Jenkins told you?" she

asked softly. "About the 'big bargain'?"

"Why, yes, child," he answered, putting his hand on her head. "Why should I doubt him? He had the proof with him, didn't he?"

"What are you getting at?" Jim asked. He and the other Bob-Whites clustered around her, waiting to hear what she had to say. "Don't you think Jenkins is on the level?"

"No, I don't believe him for one minute!" Trixie replied confidently. "And I'll tell you why. Did you take a good look at that box, Mr. Carver?"

"Why, no," he said, "as a matter of fact, I didn't. I just saw that it was old and rusty, as though it had been exposed to the damp for a long time."

"There's more to it than that," Trixie said. "It was a box that some kind of patent medicine originally came in, and on the cover, way down at the bottom, in little letters, it said, 'Patented in 1908.' So how could Ruth have hidden the necklace in it before the Civil War in 1861?"

"Maybe Jenkins just used that box to put the emeralds in to bring over here," Di suggested.

"No, I don't think so," Trixie insisted. "Remember he said, 'This is the box I found at Rosewood Hall'?"

"That's right, he did," Brian said. "Then how do you figure he found the emeralds?"

"I was just coming to that," Trixie answered, taking a deep breath. "In the first place, the necklace in that box was nothing like the one Ruth was wearing in the picture in the locket!"

"I don't remember it very clearly," Mr. Carver said. "Get me the locket, will you, Jim? I want to have another look."

Jim brought the gold heart from the desk drawer and handed it to him.

"You're right, Trixie!" he said excitedly. "It isn't the same!"

"Well, how do you know the necklace in the picture is the same one we're hunting for?" Mart asked.

"We don't, for sure," Trixie admitted, "but I assumed it was the same one, because the locket was a Christmas present to Ruth, and the emeralds had a special association with Christmas. Remember, they were supposed to be worn at that time every year."

"That's just supposition again," Brian said. "I'm sorry to burst your balloon, Sis, but you've got to have better proof than that, I'm afraid."

"Well, it just so happens I have," Trixie answered, a smug look on her face. "You see, the necklace that Jenkins showed us was just a piece of junk jewelry!"

"Are you sure?" Mr. Carver asked, his hands gripping the arms of his chair until the knuckles showed white.

"Of course I'm sure!" Trixie said. "Didn't you think so, too?" she asked, turning to Di and Honey.

"I thought so, but I didn't trust my own judgment," Di said.

"It's just like the costume jewelry they sell in any department store," Honey said. "It's *good* junk jewelry, if you know what I mean, but it certainly isn't *real*. There's a different look to real stones."

"Why didn't you say something when Jenkins was here?" Mart asked impatiently.

"Well, Trixie gave us the high sign," Di said, "so we just pretended to admire it, too."

"Well, what do you know!" Mart cried. "Leave it to the girls to know a genuine 'jool' when they see it!"

"What was Jenkins's idea of trying to palm off something like that on Mr. Carver?" Di asked, looking puzzled.

"Oh, it's simple," Trixie said. "He wanted to draw a red herring across our trail, so he'd have more time to look for the real necklace."

"That's right," Brian agreed. "He probably thought Mr. Carver, like a lot of dumb males, wouldn't know whether they were fake or not, and he obviously didn't expect to find anyone else here who might question them."

"What did he say when he phoned you yesterday?" Trixie asked Mr. Carver.

"Well, I must say, it was a rather strange conversation," he replied. "He started out by saying he was sorry about my accident and asked if I was all right again. I wondered how he knew about it, and then today when he came in, I had an uncomfortable feeling that he had been right here in this room before."

"Oh, I've had that sensation," Mart said. "Sometimes you'll be doing something, and all of a sudden you're sure you've been in exactly that same situation before. It's kind of eerie, isn't it?"

"Yes, it is," Mr. Carver said, his brows wrinkled in thought, "particularly since, so far as I know, Jenkins has never been in Green Trees. My lawyer handled all the details of the sale of Rosewood from his office, so there was no need of our meeting here."

"Well, try not to worry about it, Mr. Carver," Trixie said reassuringly. "The important thing is that we didn't fall into his trap."

"You're right, Trixie," he said, smiling down at her, "and we mustn't forget you have some unfinished business to attend to. I hope the secret staircase is aired out by now. Let's go in right now and see if the fan was any help."

"Now, you take it easy!" Brian warned Trixie as she got ready to go down the circular stairs. "If you begin to feel the least bit out of breath, you come back."

"I promise," Trixie answered as she took the flashlight and disappeared into the opening.

"The air's a lot fresher today," she called back after she had taken several steps down. "I don't think I'll have a bit of trouble."

Everyone heaved a sigh of relief at that and then waited in silent expectation for several minutes. Finally Jim couldn't stand it another second. He called to see if she was all right.

"Yes, and I think I've finally got to the bottom!" Her voice came back muffled but strong. Then, soon after, "There's an opening down here, and it looks as if it goes into a tunnel!"

"Don't take any chances!" Jim shouted to her.

"I won't, but I'm going on in," Trixie called back. "Don't worry if you don't hear me for a little while. I'll be back soon."

There was another period of anxious waiting, and then the Bob-Whites and Mr. Carver heard her coming back up the stairs. As soon as she poked her head out into the room, they knew that she had discovered the secret passage!

"It's there! It's there!" she cried, her eyes shining. "A tunnel big enough to stand up in, all made of brick!"

"Hurrah for Trixie!" Mart cried as Jim grabbed her and swung her around. It was a wild scene for several minutes. Then Trixie happened to glance in the direction of the door to the hall, and there, looking like a thundercloud, stood Miss Bates!

"Great day in the morning! Just what's the meaning of this uproar?" she asked, looking at Trixie stormily. "What did Edgar mean when he said you weren't the obstreperous kind? And him with that grievous head wound, too. You should be absolutely ashamed of yourselves!"

She was talking so fast that no one had a chance to interrupt her until she ran out of breath and was forced to stop. Then Mr. Carver rolled his chair over to her and, motioning her to come in, said with a laugh, "Oh, Carolyn, you couldn't be more wrong! Relax! We were just having a little celebration."

"Celebration!" she repeated angrily, looking around the room. "You call it a celebration, when these young hoodlums break this priceless paneling and make so much noise that you couldn't even hear when I knocked on the door? Celebration, indeed!"

She was so furious that she was shaking, and only when she noticed the bowl of custard starting to slip out of her basket did she stop her tirade. By this time, Edgar Carver was laughing uproariously. That only made Miss Bates more furious.

"Please, Miss Bates," Trixie said softly, "I'm sorry we were so noisy, but we *were* pretty excited. You see, we finally found the secret passage."

This was almost more than Carolyn Bates could stand. She looked from Trixie to Mr. Carver in complete disbelief, and then, seeing him nod his head, she sat down abruptly on a nearby love seat, not even noticing when Trixie rescued the custard by quietly taking the basket and setting it on the floor.

"That hole in the wall isn't broken paneling," Mr. Carver explained. "It's the entrance to the stairs leading down through the cellar."

"Well, I'll have to see it to believe it," Miss Bates answered, taking off her hat and gloves and getting up from the love seat.

"Would you like to go down and have a look?" Trixie asked, a mischievous smile on her face as she thought of buxom Miss Bates trying to make her way down the narrow steps.

"Good heavens, no!" Miss Bates replied, putting her head inside the open panel. "I can see it wasn't built for the likes of me! I'll have to be satisfied with

having you tell me about it. Did you figure this out
from the blueprints?"

"Well, yes and no," Trixie began cautiously, not
yet knowing whether Miss Bates's anger had really
subsided. "You see, I was puzzled, just as you were,
about those funny measurements between this room
and Mr. Carver's study, so I examined the walls in
here and noticed that this particular panel wasn't as
solid as the others."

"Yes, yes, go on," Miss Bates urged, leaning forward expectantly.

"And then I felt along the moldings until I discovered this little depression." Trixie pulled the panel
down so she could show Miss Bates what she was
talking about. "You see, it goes up and down just like
a window."

Miss Bates moved the panel several times, as
though to convince herself that it really worked as
Trixie had said.

"My dear," she said, holding out her hand, "I
apologize! You're a smart girl. With all the work I've
done on old houses, it would never have occurred to
me that a staircase could be built in such a small
area. Now, go on, and tell me more about what's
down below."

Trixie explained how the steps evidently had been
built inside one of the huge piers that supported the
house, going down below the cellar floor level and
connecting with a subterranean tunnel.

"Have you gone all the way through it?" Miss Bates

asked, her eyes bright with excitement.

"No, I had just come back to tell Mr. Carver what I'd found, when you came in," Trixie said, "but I mean to go back and look for—" an almost imperceptible warning sign from Jim made her hesitate before she went on—"look for the opening at the other end."

She was so excited that she had almost disclosed the secret of the emeralds, but she had caught herself in time.

"I do wish I could stay and hear about what you find," Miss Bates said, "but I have to meet the architect who is working on the old Bailey house, and I don't want to give him the satisfaction of telling me I'm late. May I come back tomorrow, Edgar, or am I wearing out my welcome?"

"You know you are always welcome, Carolyn," he said warmly as he started to escort her into the hall.

Miss Bates suddenly remembered her basket. Picking it up, she handed it to Honey, asking that she be sure to see that Edgar ate the custard. "The other dish," she explained, "contains the poultice, which should be heated and put on his head."

Edgar Carver thanked her for the custard, but Trixie noticed he made no promises about using the poultice. She knew that he had long ago become accustomed to his friend Carolyn's whims.

The Green Trees Ghost · 16

NATURALLY the Bob-Whites were impatient to see the secret tunnel. While they were waiting for Mr. Carver to return from showing Miss Bates to the door, they decided that each one should make a trip down the circular staircase.

"If one of you happens to see the brick marked with an X when you're in the tunnel, just give the Bob-White signal," Trixie suggested, "but don't waste a lot of time looking for it."

"We know what you're getting at," Mart laughed. "You just don't want any of us stealing your thunder. You want to find the emeralds all by yourself, don't you?"

The inquiry was good-natured, but Trixie was furious. She made a flying leap toward her brother, but Jim managed to catch her by the shoulders. Turning to Mart, he said, "I think you'd better take that crack back, Mart, old boy. After all, it's Trixie who's got this close to the solution, so I can't say I blame her for wanting to go on with it, can you?"

"Sorry, Trix; honest I am," Mart apologized, his face reddening.

It wasn't often that any of the Bob-Whites interfered when he teased his sister, but Mart knew that this time he had gone a little too far. Trixie, quickly sensing the sincerity of his apology, forced back her anger.

"Jeepers, Mart," she said, "I should know you well enough by now not to let you make me mad. But sometimes—sometimes you just get my goat!"

The little scene was interrupted when the Bob-Whites heard the phone ring in Mr. Carver's study, and it wasn't long before he came wheeling back into the music room.

"It was your father, Di," he said, excitement sounding in his voice. "He and Mrs. Lynch would like to come over and see Green Trees, and he suggested we all have lunch with them afterward."

"Oh, that's wonderful!" Di said enthusiastically. "I've been wanting them to see the house, but Daddy's been so busy with all those old meetings that he hasn't had time."

"Now that you mention lunch, I realize I'm starving," Mart said, hugging his middle with both arms. "We were so excited, we forgot about food."

"That's the first time I've ever known *you* to forget *eats!*" Brian teased.

"Well, we could have resorted to dear Carolyn's custard," Mr. Carver said with a twinkle in his eye, "but Mr. Lynch's invitation sounds much more appealing. Can you take a little time out from your investigations, Trixie? I think you need a short break."

Trixie's heart sank. She wasn't the least bit interested in food. All she wanted was to get back into the passage and look for the X-marked brick. It was hard enough to have to wait until everyone had had a chance to see what the tunnel looked like, and now another delay! It occurred to her that she might suggest that they go to lunch without her, but she quickly vetoed this idea. She knew it would be impolite to Mr. Carver, who was anticipating meeting the Lynches with such obvious pleasure. She couldn't throw a wet blanket on the party by not going along.

Swallowing her disappointment and making an effort to sound enthusiastic, she said, "An hour or two won't make any difference, Mr. Carver. After all, the necklace has been hidden for a good many years, so I guess it won't run away by itself now."

"Good girl, Trixie," Jim said under his breath as he came over to her. "Don't think I don't know how hard that was for you."

By the time the Bob-Whites had freshened up, Mr. Carver had changed into a white linen suit and gone to the front door to watch for the visitors. It was quite apparent that he was unusually excited at the chance to show Green Trees to someone who he knew had a special interest in it and more than ordinary appreciation of its beauty.

When Mr. and Mrs. Lynch arrived, the two men greeted each other warmly, and Mrs. Lynch, looking pretty and cool in a pale yellow dress, shook hands with Edgar Carver.

"After all we've heard about you from the Bob-Whites," she said, "introductions seem scarcely necessary. We don't feel like strangers."

"That is true," he replied, "and I've been waiting for the time when I could welcome you to Green Trees. Suppose I take you through the house, and then I'll let Trixie bring you up to date on our latest discoveries."

"A splendid idea!" Mr. Lynch answered. "If I weren't so anxious to see these beautiful rooms, I'm afraid my curiosity about what those six have been up to would get the better of me."

"We'll meet you later, back in the music room," Trixie said. "We have several things to do, so take your time."

Once back at the entrance to the circular staircase Trixie, wanting to be perfectly fair about who should go first, repeated the old counting-out rhyme her mother had taught her years before.

"Intry, mintry, cutry, corn. Apple seed and apple thorn. Wire, briar, limber, lock. Six geese in a flock. One flew east, one flew west, and one flew over the cuckoo's nest."

When it worked out that Di was to go first, she drew back timidly.

"Honestly, Trix," she said, "I'm scared to death to go down there alone. Can't Mart come with me?"

"Well, the stairs are too narrow for more than one to go down at a time," Trixie answered understandingly, "but Mart can go first and wait for you in the tunnel. There's more room once you get in there."

Mart was only too glad to have the chance to see the secret passage, and Di, her courage now fortified by his presence, followed him through the open panel. It wasn't long before they were back, however, a disquieting look on their faces.

"What's the matter, Di?" Trixie asked. "You look as though you'd seen a ghost."

"And, Mart, you look a little green, too," Brian added. "What happened?"

"Remember what Mr. Carver said about the Green Trees ghost?" Mart asked. "Well, we didn't see it, but we sure heard it!"

"Yes," Di continued breathlessly. "We were just a little way inside the tunnel when we heard something tap-tap-tapping, just the way Mr. Carver said the stonemason's ghost did. I don't think we ought to go one step further with this crazy hunt, do you?" She looked anxiously from one to the other of the Bob-Whites.

"Oh, come on!" Trixie cried. "You don't *really* think that was a ghost, do you?"

"It wasn't just an ordinary ghost," Mart said, his eyes bright with excitement. "It was an honest-to-goodness poltergeist! That's what it was!"

"A *what?*" Honey asked.

"A poltergeist!" Mart repeated. "That's a ghost who makes a lot of noise to call attention to himself, and I've read of any number of cases where people have heard them."

"Well, poltergeist or just plain ghost, I, for one, don't take any stock in them," Trixie said positively. "I'm going back into that tunnel and see if I can find out what it was you heard, because I have a feeling you *did* hear something."

"You're not going in there alone, ghosts or no ghosts!" Jim said. "I'll come along. In fact, this time I insist on going first, Miss Belden."

Trixie didn't argue. Seeming a little relieved at Jim's decision, she handed him the flashlight that Mart had given her when he and Di returned.

"Be absolutely quiet, Jim," she whispered as they reached the entrance to the tunnel and started making their way through it.

There wasn't a sound to be heard for some time, and then Trixie tapped Jim on the shoulder and said under her breath, "Listen!"

They could hear definite sounds of a rapping, then a grating noise, such as a trowel might make on stone, but there was no sign of life or light ahead of them.

"Keep going," Trixie whispered tensely, pushing

Jim ahead of her down the passageway.

They proceeded, inch by inch, for some time, until suddenly the flashlight revealed an obstruction in their path. It turned out to be a pile of dirt and bricks, completely blocking the passage. They could go no farther. Something, sometime, had caused this part of the tunnel to cave in. Again they listened in silence, and again they heard the same noises from the other side of the rubble.

At a sign from Trixie, they started to retrace their steps. When they had gone partway, Trixie whispered to Jim, "*Now* I know that ghost! It's Jenkins, digging on the other side! Let's get out of here as fast as we can! We've got work to do!"

When they returned to the music room, they found Mr. and Mrs. Lynch and Mr. Carver waiting for them. Di's father was inspecting the panel with great interest.

"This is a unique house," he said as Trixie and Jim emerged, "and Di tells us she and Mart heard the specter of the mason, which only adds to its fascination. Did you hear it, too, Trixie?" His jocular manner indicated that he, too, was skeptical about the ghost, and Trixie noticed that Di and Mart now seemed much more relaxed.

"No, it wasn't a ghost," she replied, "but I almost wish it had been!"

"What do you mean?" Honey asked. "You *did* hear something?"

"Yes." Jim continued the story. "We heard the

same tapping sounds and noises—as though someone were digging. Trixie thinks it was Jenkins. You see, the tunnel is blocked up halfway through, so we couldn't tell for sure."

"It looks to me, Trixie," Mr. Lynch said, his voice becoming serious, "as if Jenkins is as confident as you that the *real* necklace—" He paused at Trixie's startled expression. "Yes," he continued, "Mr. Carver told me about the trick Jenkins tried to pull with the phony emeralds. But what puzzles me is how he could have known about the tunnel and the marked brick."

"Well, you see," Trixie began, glancing at Mr. Carver, "we think he stole the directions Ruth left in the locket."

"Why, you didn't tell me you suspected anything like that," Edgar Carver interposed. "You mean—" He started to speak again, and then a strange expression swept over his face. "Wait a minute! Everything is beginning to come back to me. That day I fell out of the chair. He was here! I remember now, and he threatened me when I wouldn't give him the locket. Everything after that is a complete blank, until I came to on the sofa, with Brian bandaging my head."

"We suspected something like that, Mr. Carver," Brian said. "Trixie found the locket with the paper missing the morning you were hurt, but we didn't want to worry you about Jenkins unless we had to."

"That was most considerate of you," Edgar Carver said softly. "I only wish I could help you hunt for the marked brick. Time is running out for you, and now you have that man literally breathing down your necks. Have you any suggestions, sir?" he asked Mr. Lynch. "You're leaving tomorrow, aren't you?"

"Your question brings me to something I was going to tell you during lunch," Mr. Lynch said with a smile. "Mrs. Lynch and I have fallen in love with this part of the country, and during the last few days I have been making some inquiries about Rosewood Hall. I found that Jenkins's scheme to start a horse farm isn't working out very well, and he's only too willing to sell."

"You mean you're going to buy it, Daddy?" Di asked eagerly.

"Yes, dear. I've looked over the property, and this morning the papers were signed. I hope to rebuild Rosewood just as it was originally," Mr. Lynch said. "I can see now why Jenkins was so eager to sell and get out of the neighborhood."

"Yes," Trixie mused, "he probably thought he could sell the imitation necklace to Mr. Carver, discover the real emeralds, and clear out before anyone heard about it and tried to stop him."

"Unquestionably, the man is a scoundrel," Mr. Lynch agreed, "so I'd advise you to carry on your search without delay. We'll have to stay on for a day or so longer than we first planned, to wind up the details of the purchase, so you don't need to worry about having to leave for home, Trixie. But you *do* have to worry about Jenkins beating you to the treasure! I don't take legal possession of Rosewood until tomorrow, so, you see, I can't yet order him off the property."

"Your acquisition of Rosewood is certainly exciting news!" Edgar Carver said warmly. "I shall not only be extremely glad to get rid of Jenkins, but also I shall welcome having you as a neighbor."

"Thank you, sir," Mr. Lynch replied cordially. "I don't know how much time I'll be able to spend here, but I hope to vacation at Rosewood as often as I can." Then, glancing at Trixie, he continued, "But I can see Trixie is impatient to get back to the secret passage. Shall we go to lunch right now and not lose any more time?"

Trixie suddenly decided she would *have* to change her mind about going to lunch with the others. Even an hour might make the difference between success and failure, and now that Mr. Carver and the Lynches knew about the strange noises in the tunnel, she felt they would understand her decision.

"Honestly, Mr. Lynch," she said, "I couldn't eat a thing right now. Would you think I was terribly impolite if I just stayed here and went on hunting?"

"Not at all. Not at all," he replied, "if Jim will stay with you. You may need some help, you know."

"Of course I'll stay," Jim was quick to reply. "Come on, Trix, let's get going!"

"Just a minute, me hearties," Mart interrupted, in his best imitation of an English accent. "What about the rest of us? If you coves think you're going to pull this caper without me, you're dotty!" He turned to the other Bob-Whites. "Right, chaps?"

It was Brian, the eldest, who made the decision.

"Look, Mart," he said understandingly. "I know how you feel, and Honey and Di, too, for that matter. We'd all like to go to the end of the trail, but there's just so much space below stairs to work in, so what could we really do to help?" He looked around for confirmation. "I move we appoint Trixie and Jim to go on with the hunt, while the rest of us go to lunch. What do you say?"

For a moment there was silence. Then Mart broke it with a groan.

"Why did you have to mention food, dear brother of mine? You knew what I'd say." Turning to the girls he went on cheerily, "No adventurer I, when the dinner bell rings. Let's go eat!"

Mart's humor and good nature were infectious. As the group broke up and started for the door, they were all laughing.

"Good luck!" Mr. Carver called back to Trixie and Jim as he left with the others for Williamsburg and the Inn.

Jim and Trixie, alone now, descended into the familiar depths of the stairwell.

"I don't think Ruth would pick a spot that was too hard to find, do you?" Trixie asked as they approached the tunnel. "Or is that just wishful thinking?"

"No, she probably worked out the intricate plan for hiding the directions in the urn so no one except her sister would find them," Jim said, "and then she would have chosen a brick in plain sight. There'd have been no reason to make it too difficult once Ruth had got into the secret passage."

"Well, I hope you're right," Trixie sighed. "Suppose we start going down the right-hand side. You hold the flashlight over my shoulder."

Trixie began running her hands over the bricks, one by one, occasionally stopping to scratch the moss away when she thought she felt an indentation. She tried not to let her growing feeling of frustration get the better of her, but, as time wore on, she became more and more discouraged.

"I'll simply die if it's hidden in the part that's caved in, or on the other side," she whispered to Jim as they neared the blocked-up end of the tunnel.

"It could be, of course," Jim answered, "but don't give up yet, Trixie. We still have the opposite wall to examine."

As they turned and started to look at the left-hand side of the tunnel, the light suddenly flashed on a brick different in texture and color from the others. It looked as though it had been waxed, and there was no moss on it. Trixie let out a gasp when she looked closely and saw a distinct X cut quite deeply into the center of the soft clay brick. It was all she could do to suppress a scream. She stuck her fingernails into the crack and tried to pry the brick loose. When it refused to budge, she turned to Jim, a desperate look on her face. Jim handed her the flashlight and, taking a small jackknife from his pocket, started to probe around the edges of the brick.

"Thank goodness it isn't set in mortar," he whispered, "but in dirt and sand. It should come out without too much trouble."

All this time, sounds of activity on the other side of the pile could be heard. The sounds became more and more distinct, and Trixie was sure Jenkins was shoveling away the rubble faster to get to their side.

"Hurry, Jim, please!" she urged. "He's coming right through here, I *know!*"

Jim worked desperately to force the brick out, but the blade was so short it didn't penetrate much.

"Do you want me to get a knife from the kitchen?" Trixie asked.

"No, thanks, I've almost got it," Jim answered, twisting the knife this way and that. "Hold the flash closer, Trix. I can't see what I'm doing."

"I've got it as close as I can, Jim," Trixie whispered.

They had been so preoccupied that neither of them noticed the light growing dimmer and dimmer. Then suddenly it went out completely, leaving them in utter darkness!

"Oh, Jim! What will we do?" she moaned, giving the flashlight a desperate shake to see if it had any more life in it. "The batteries are completely dead, but we can't leave now!"

"Wait a minute, Trix," Jim said. "The brick is so loose it's practically out. Here, change places with me. Maybe your fingers are small enough to pry it out of the wall now."

Feeling her way, Trixie reached between the bricks, where the crack felt widest, and, with a desperate effort and a silent prayer, she pulled. Suddenly the brick came out and fell to the floor with a dull thud. The sound of Jenkins's digging stopped abruptly, and Trixie's heart skipped a beat as she and Jim waited to see what would happen. After what seemed an eternity, the noises started up again, and Trixie cautiously reached into the open space where the brick had been. She felt something cold. With shaking hands, she lifted out what she was sure was a small metal box.

"Come on, Jim," she said under her breath. "Let's get out of here. I think we've come to the end of the trail!"

They felt their way along the wall of the tunnel to the bottom of the stairs, where the light from above, dim though it was, let them see well enough.

Once back in the music room, the first thing Trixie did was to pull the panel down.

"I don't want to run the risk of Jenkins's coming through there," she explained. "He just might dig his way through that barrier."

"Come on into the study," Jim suggested, noticing that Trixie's face was unnaturally pale and that, despite the heat of the day, she was shivering. "It'll be more comfortable in there, and you look as though you need to sit down for a while."

He took her gently by the hand and led her out, Trixie still clutching the unopened box.

The First to Know • 17

Trixie slumped into a chair near the window, where the warm sunlight poured in.

"It does feel good to relax," she said. "I'm glad it's all over. I feel as though I'd been on the jump for days."

"I won't believe the hunt is over until I actually see the necklace, Trix," Jim said. "Go on; open the box."

"No, Jim," she answered slowly. "Don't think I'm not just as anxious as you are to see what's in it, but I've been thinking."

She paused, looking out across the stretch of lawn toward the old burying ground. Jim didn't hurry her. He sensed that she was preoccupied with a decision that she had to make herself.

"Jim," she finally began again, "I don't think Ruth would have wanted a complete stranger to open this box. She hid it for her sister, and, since she's not here, I feel Mr. Carver should be the one. Do you see what I mean?"

"Of course I do," Jim said. "You know, Trix, people may say you're impulsive, but when it comes to something really important, you're the most thoughtful person I've ever known."

Trixie thanked her lucky stars that Jim was standing in back of her so he couldn't see the telltale blush she knew was flooding her face. She couldn't say a word.

Mart came running in ahead of the others, holding a big paper bag high over his head.

"Belden catering service!" he shouted. "Double hamburgers and french fries, coming up!"

"And chocolate malts!" Honey, who was just behind him with Di and Brian, held up two tall plastic containers.

"Anything new, Trix?" Brian asked eagerly.

Trixie shook her head enigmatically. She didn't want to spoil the surprise for all of them when she told Mr. Carver of her discovery. "Be patient while I eat. I'm starved, and I can't talk with my mouth full, you know," she chuckled, hoping to put them off.

When Trixie smelled the delicious odor of food, she suddenly realized how hungry she was. She unobtrusively pushed the metal box under the chair cushion for the time being. As Mart handed her the big juicy hamburger, he told her that Mr. Carver was

giving the Lynches a glimpse of the formal gardens
but they would be along in a few minutes.

Just as Trixie and Jim had finished eating, Mr. and
Mrs. Lynch and Edgar Carver came in. As soon as
Mr. Carver entered the room, he wheeled his chair
over to Trixie. There was no need for him to speak.
The question in his eyes was there for all of them to
see. Trixie started to reach under the cushion for the
box, when the silent tableau was shattered.

"Mr. Lynch! You!" It was Jenkins. He stood, the
picture of shocked surprise, in the French doors,
confronting Di's father.

"Yes, Mr. Jenkins, it is indeed I," Mr. Lynch replied coldly, motioning the man to come in. Jenkins
looked as though he wanted to turn tail and run.
But, twisting his hat in his hands and looking from
one to the other of the Bob-Whites, he slowly came
in and sat on the edge of the chair which Brian
pushed toward him. Trixie noticed there was brick
dust on the knees of his riding breeches and in his
short-cropped hair. He apparently had come here
directly from the tunnel.

"I just dropped in to see Mr. Carver," he began,
his voice sounding unnaturally loud as he tried to
regain his composure. "I didn't expect to find *you*
here."

"I'm sure you didn't," Mr. Lynch replied. "I'm
Diana's father," he went on, "and these are her
friends. I take it you've met them."

"Yes, sir," Jenkins said, his tone somewhat meeker,

"but Mr. Carver didn't tell me their last names."

Edgar Carver edged his wheelchair into the circle as Jenkins finished speaking.

"Yesterday," he said icily, "you came here with a necklace you purportedly found at Rosewood. Seeing what I believed to be a family heirloom naturally upset me emotionally, and it didn't occur to me then to question your veracity."

Jenkins stood up. His attempt to smile ended in failure.

"Oh," he whined, "I didn't mean to have you on, Mr. Carver. I just thought—"

"You just thought you'd take advantage of a situation you happened to stumble on," Mr. Carver charged angrily, "and had it not been for Trixie, you might very likely have succeeded."

"But I never said I'd found the necklace at Rosewood." Jenkins's whine was even more pronounced. "You can't get anything on me. I said I'd found the *box* over there, and that was the truth. I found it in the loft over the stable."

"Now, wait a minute," Mr. Lynch interposed. "We're not interested in 'getting' anything on you, although I'm sure that, with a little police work, there would be plenty of evidence against you. Mr. Carver discussed this whole thing with me."

He paused to let Jenkins get the full impact of his words before continuing.

"I'm sure you won't deny you came to Green Trees looking for information about the necklace. In the course of your visit, Mr. Carver fell and injured himself. We strongly suspect that this was when he tried to keep you from stealing the directions to the treasure."

Jenkins started to say something, but Mr. Lynch silenced him with an upraised hand.

"When you learned from Neil that Mr. Carver remembered nothing of the affair, you came back and tried to swindle him. This is enough to put you behind bars for a long time, but all we want is for you to get out of town. I'll give you twenty-four hours. If you're in the neighborhood after that, I'll have the police pick you up!"

Jenkins looked from Mr. Lynch to Mr. Carver, then cast a frightened glance at the circle of Bob-Whites.

"I—I—" he began. Then he whirled and ran out of the room. The last they saw of him, he was driving up the road, away from Rosewood Hall and Green Trees, in an ancient pickup truck.

The Bob-Whites breathed a sigh of relief when he had gone. Edgar Carver was visibly shaken, and the tight lines around Mr. Lynch's mouth showed that his anger had not yet subsided.

"I don't think I've ever in my life seen a more unsavory character!" Mrs. Lynch burst out. "I hope he never shows his face around here again!"

"I don't think you have to worry about that, Mother," Mr. Lynch assured her. "His kind know when it's getting too hot for them; they move out like rats leaving a sinking ship."

"I'm not concerned about *him*," Honey said. "What's been worrying me are the horses at Rosewood. Who'll take care of them, with Jenkins and Neil both gone?"

"Gleeps!" Trixie suddenly exclaimed. "I've got an idea. Why couldn't Neil go back to Rosewood Hall, Mr. Lynch, now that Jenkins isn't there?"

"That's certainly a possibility," Mr. Lynch replied. "I'll suggest it this afternoon when he comes to see me."

"Oh, that would be just perfect," Trixie said. "He loves horses, and maybe he could start back to school in the fall, too."

"That's quite possible," Mr. Lynch went on. "I want to find a competent overseer for the place, so Neil wouldn't have the whole responsibility. It should work out very well."

Trixie was dying to tell Mr. Carver about the box. Now, with everyone relaxed again after Jenkins's departure and warmed by the solution of Neil's problem, she knew the moment had arrived.

"Well, child," Mr. Carver said softly, "I never got to ask how you and Jim fared this morning. Now I'm almost afraid to press you for an answer."

Trixie glanced at Jim, then at the others. She slipped the little silver box from under the chair cushion, stood up, and, taking a step forward, laid it in Edgar Carver's lap.

"When you open this, you'll be the first to know

whether we were successful or not," she said, her
voice trembling with emotion.

"You mean—" Mr. Carver paused, incredulous.
"You mean you haven't looked to see what's in here?"

"No, sir," Jim said. "I was all for opening it right
away, but Trixie said she wanted to wait for you."

"Thank you, Trixie, my dear," was all he said. His
voice was barely audible.

Trixie stood beside his chair, almost afraid to look
as he removed the cover from the tarnished silver
box. Inside was a piece of black velvet. He carefully
lifted out the cloth and, after handing the box back
to Trixie, unfolded it. Just at that moment, the rays
of the late afternoon sun fell across his chair, lending
their light to the dazzling brilliance of the emeralds
that lay revealed on his lap. A gasp went up from
everyone as they clustered close around Mr. Carver
to admire the beautiful necklace.

His eyes were shining as he lifted up the gems and
insisted that each one have a chance to examine them
personally.

"This must be worth a fortune!" Mrs. Lynch exclaimed as she held the necklace up to her throat
and admired the effect in the mirror over the mantel.
Then, turning to Mr. Carver, she said, "I'm sorry.
I didn't mean to sound mercenary. Naturally, a
family heirloom's value to you is wholly sentimental,
isn't it?"

Trixie waited intently to hear what his reply to this
rather casual question might be.

While everyone's attention had been focused on the necklace, she had been doing some serious thinking. Whether the plan that had suddenly occurred to her might be possible depended a great deal on Mr. Carver's answer.

His reply came slowly. He had been sitting with bowed head, running the palms of his hands over his knees. Then he glanced at Trixie and took a deep breath.

"I suppose if I had a family, I would be *very* sentimental about the necklace, Mrs. Lynch," he said. "I would want the tradition to be carried on. I can see, in my mind's eye, a festive Christmas here at Green Trees—like the ones when I was a child—complete with mistletoe and holly and someone dear to me wearing the emeralds. But I'm alone, the last of the Carver line, and I feel very strongly that if these stones ever had a charm or a curse, now is the time to break it."

Everyone leaned forward as Edgar Carver spoke. Trixie's heart was pounding as she waited for him to continue.

"If Alex still thinks it possible for me to walk again, I intend to sell the emeralds right away and have the operation!"

"Just what I hoped! Just what I hoped!" Trixie cried. "Of course you can walk again, Mr. Carver! I *know* you can! I've never been so happy in my whole life!"

Her enthusiasm was infectious, and Mr. Carver

positively glowed under the warmth of everyone's
encouragement. Di and Honey, half laughing and
half crying, embraced each other. Brian and Mart
found themselves shaking hands, and Jim and Trixie
just looked at each other, Trixie not too far from
tears herself. Mr. and Mrs. Lynch surveyed the
moving scene with sympathetic approval. It was
Edgar Carver who brought them all back to earth
again.

"Alex told me it will take several months after
the operation to strengthen the muscles in these old
legs," he said cheerily. "I'll have to exercise like the
very dickens, but I'll do anything to walk again!"

"Edgar, what was that you said about walking
again?"

It was Miss Bates. She had come up to the terrace
just in time to catch his last words. Trixie ran to the
door to meet her.

"Yes, Miss Bates," she cried. "We found the necklace, and Mr. Carver's going to have the operation,
and Mr. Lynch is going to—"

The words tumbled out in wild profusion and
stopped only when Miss Carolyn, waving her pink
parasol menacingly over Trixie's head, called for
silence.

"Great day in the morning!" she exclaimed. "Every
time I come into this house, I find you all in an
uproar. Edgar, will you be so kind as to explain
what this child is trying to tell me?"

Trixie laughed good-humoredly, for she had caught

the twinkle in Miss Bates's eye and knew that this tirade was just a matter of habit.

"First let me introduce Mr. and Mrs. Lynch," Edgar Carver said, "Di's parents. Miss Bates is my old and dear friend."

"I do declare!" Carolyn Bates said, sweeping over to take Mrs. Lynch's hand. "I thought you looked familiar. We met briefly at one of the meetings in Williamsburg, didn't we?"

"We did indeed," Mrs. Lynch replied warmly. "How nice to see you again!"

Miss Bates plumped down on the sofa, and Trixie held her breath as she heard the springs squeak menacingly at the unaccustomed weight.

"Come, come, Edgar," Miss Bates said. "No more stalling. What was Trixie trying to say about the necklace?"

"So much has happened since you were here yesterday, I scarcely know where to begin," he replied. "Yes, Trixie found the emeralds, and here they are."

He handed the box to Miss Bates, its cover opened to show the jewels nestled in the black velvet. She took a long look at them and started to speak, but for once words failed her.

"Aren't they beautiful?" Trixie exclaimed, breaking the silence.

"They're more than beautiful," Miss Bates finally said. "They are exquisite, and about as useful as a pink elephant! What do you propose to do with them, Edgar?"

Everyone in the room was completely taken aback at this reaction to Trixie's discovery—everyone, that is, except Edgar Carver, who looked as if her question pleased him.

"Dear Carolyn," he said affectionately, "I knew I could count on your practical good sense. I intend to sell the necklace and—" He paused, as though not quite sure how his old friend would accept the rest of his plan.

"Yes, yes, go on," she urged him.

"And, if it's not too late, I'm going to see if they can patch up my back so I can walk again."

"At last!" Miss Carolyn cried. "At last the man is coming to his senses!" She turned to Mr. and Mrs. Lynch. "For years we who have been closest to Edgar have been trying to get him to do this, but he's been as stubborn as—" She glanced at Mr. Carver and, leaving the sentence hanging in midair, got up and walked over to him. Taking his hands in hers, she went on softly. "But all that doesn't matter now. The important thing is that you're finally able to have the operation—and, Trixie, the credit is all yours!"

"Oh, I don't *want* any credit, Miss Bates," Trixie said. "It's enough to know that the necklace will do him some good. Besides, I couldn't have done a thing without the other Bob-Whites."

Mr. Lynch had been watching this scene with much interest, and now he interrupted it by saying, with a glance at his watch, that, much as he hated to leave, he had to return to the motel in the village in time for his appointment with Neil.

"We never did get to tell you that I have bought Rosewood Hall," he said, addressing Miss Bates, "and I certainly hope you will help me with its reconstruction when the time comes."

"I heard rumors that you'd purchased it," she replied with a smile. "News spreads fast around here, and I'm glad it's true. Just think, Rosewood Hall and Green Trees can be the Twin Houses again." She sighed. "I'll do everything I can to help. I love them both!"

As the group broke up, Honey suggested that the Bob-Whites go over to the Rosewood stables and check on the horses.

"Jenkins may not have left them any water or feed," she said. "I can't sleep tonight without being sure they're all right."

"That's a good idea," Mr. Carver said, "and I'd like to make another suggestion. I'd like all of you to come back tomorrow evening for a little farewell party. I'll get Alex, and I'd like to have Neil, too. It's high time he and I met, if we're going to be neighbors."

Everyone eagerly accepted his gracious invitation, at the same time offering to help with the arrangements for the party.

"Suppose you leave them to Mrs. Lynch and me," Miss Bates said. "Men don't know about such things. Do you agree?" she asked, turning expectantly to Di's mother.

"I agree to help in whatever way I can—" Mrs. Lynch laughed—"and I also agree that most parties do need a woman's touch."

"I give up!" Mr. Carver said. "I've known Carolyn too long to cross her, so I'll relax and enjoy my own party. Until tomorrow, then."

Happy, Happy Birthday! • 18

THE BOB-WHITES, after arranging to meet Mr. and Mrs. Lynch in time for dinner, strolled across the lawn to Rosewood Hall.

"Doesn't it seem funny to be able just to walk in?" Trixie commented as they made their way to the stables.

"I'm dying to see the horses!" Honey exclaimed. "The one Jenkins was riding the other day looked like a thoroughbred."

"I know," Brian said, "but after what Neil told Trixie about the way Jenkins treated them, I'm wondering what shape they'll be in."

They found the dilapidated stables a sad contrast to the beautiful ones Honey's father maintained in Sleepyside. The doors were sagging, some of the broken windows had been stuffed with bits of burlap, and the roof was badly in need of new shingles. It was with real trepidation that they went through a small side door hanging ajar on one hinge. Soft whinnies and the sound of hooves pawing the wooden floor came from the main part of the building. Entering it, they saw that only three of the several stalls were occupied.

"Oh, you poor thing!" Trixie cried as she looked into the first space and found Honey's fears were justified. Both the water bucket and the feed trough were empty. The horse, a lovely roan, shied away from her at first, tossing his head high. She spoke softly to him, and presently he put his head down and let her rub his soft, velvety nose.

"Brian, bring some water, will you?" she asked. "And, Jim, will you and Mart look around and see if you can find the feed bins? Let's hope there's some grain left in them. These horses are hungry!"

Honey and Di, in the meantime, had been soothing the other two horses, one a black stallion with a white star between his eyes, the other a piebald mare. The boys were soon back with pails of water and a bucket of feed.

"I don't think we should give them very much at first," Trixie warned. "No knowing how long it's been since they were fed last. We don't want to run the risk of making them sick."

"You're right," Honey agreed. "We'll give them a small ration now and then come out tomorrow morning again."

"Maybe by then Neil will be able to take over,"

Jim said hopefully. "Obviously, someone has given them tender, loving care, even if Jenkins didn't. Did you notice how their coats have been curried? I'll bet that's Neil's work."

"And the saddles and harnesses are beautifully polished," Mart added, "even though they're practically worn out."

Their chores over, Trixie gave each horse a farewell pat as she went by.

"I wish we had some sugar for you," she said. "But we'll see that each of you gets some tomorrow."

They went back to Green Trees to pick up the station wagon, going by way of the gardens. The warmth of the sun had brought many of the flowers into bloom, and the air was heavy with their fragrance. A soft breeze had come up during the last hour, bringing welcome relief from the heat of the day.

"Just think," Trixie sighed, pushing back the curls which stubbornly refused to stay off her forehead, "tomorrow is our last day."

"Who would ever have thought a week ago that our trip would turn out to be so exciting?" Di said.

"You should know by now that where Trixie goes, there goes excitement!" Jim said.

"I guess if any of us wants peace and quiet, he'll have to resign from the Bob-Whites," Mart said.

"Never!" Brian cried. "United we stand, divided we'd be miserable!"

As they drove past Lizzie's store, Trixie suddenly

said, "You know, I feel bad about not being able to do something for poor Lizzie. Mr. Carver's going to walk again. Neil's back on the right track, and Rosewood's going to be saved, but I can't figure out a thing to do for Lizzie."

"You can't cure all the world's ills, Sis," Mart said affectionately. "And it isn't as though Lizzie weren't used to the kind of life she lives."

"Oh, that's not the point," Trixie said sadly. "She may be used to it, but that doesn't make it any more pleasant. You can learn how to carry a twenty-pound pack on your back, but it still weighs twenty pounds."

"Something may turn up so we can help her," Di said optimistically. "Try not to let it worry you, Trix."

They rode the rest of the way back to Williamsburg in silence, and Trixie wasn't sure whether it was because they were all so tired or whether the others were also thinking about Lizzie.

When they drove up to the cottage, they saw Neil and Mr. Lynch standing on the porch, and Trixie knew immediately, from the happy look on the boy's face, that the interview had gone well.

"Glad you got back when you did," Mr. Lynch called to them. "Neil and I have worked out a plan, and he's going back to Rosewood right away."

"Oh, Daddy!" Di cried, running up the porch steps and giving her father a hug. "Everything is working out just perfectly! The horses need Neil, and I guess Neil needs the horses!"

Before Neil left, Trixie told him how they had

watered and fed the animals.

"But we only gave them a little," Honey said, "because we didn't know when they'd been fed last, and we didn't want them to overeat."

"Don't you worry," Neil said. "I'll take care of them from now on. You wait and see!"

"I think that young man has real possibilities," Mr. Lynch observed as he watched Neil running down the road, "and you'll be interested to know there are more plans for him than he knows."

"What do you mean, Mr. Lynch?" Trixie asked him eagerly.

He told the Bob-Whites that he had received a phone call from Dr. Brandon.

"He heard about Mr. Carver's decision to have the operation and about my buying Rosewood," Mr. Lynch began. "He asked if I would help in making some of the arrangements for the trip to the hospital in New York. In the course of the discussion, Dr. Brandon said he was concerned about Mr. Carver's being alone after he returned to Green Trees, and so I—"

"You thought of Neil!" Trixie cried. "Didn't you, Mr. Lynch?"

"You're always one step ahead of me." Mr. Lynch smiled. "Yes, I thought we'd give Neil these next few weeks to prove himself at Rosewood, and if he shows that he's reliable, we'll offer him the chance to stay with Mr. Carver and help him through his long convalescence."

"You don't think Mr. Carver might like someone in the house to do the cooking and housework, do you?" Trixie ventured the question a little hesitantly.

"What are you getting at?" Mr. Lynch asked, smiling over the top of his glasses. "I suspect there's someone else you're thinking of helping. Am I right?"

"Daddy, I'm beginning to believe you're a mind reader," Di said. "Yes, it's Lizzie James she's thinking of. Isn't it, Trixie?"

"Lizzie James? Who is that?" Mr. Lynch asked.

Trixie told him about the old lady and her admiration for Mr. Carver and her courage in the face of Jenkins's threats. Mr. Lynch listened with interest and, when Trixie had finished, said that if Mr. Carver felt Lizzie might be helpful, he would stop by and see her the next day.

"Wonderful!" Trixie cried. "Now, let's hope she can cook!"

Everyone slept late the next morning, including Trixie. No one had fully realized how the events of the last few days had tired them. Rain had fallen during the night, clearing the hot, muggy atmosphere. The weather was perfect, and, since Mrs. Lynch had insisted that she didn't need their help in arranging for the party, they had the whole day to relax by the swimming pool. It was a completely lazy day—a rare experience for the Bob-Whites.

Around three o'clock, when Trixie suggested it was time they get ready for the party, Mart looked at her with an amused question in his eyes.

"Trix!" he exclaimed. "You've got two hours before we're due at Mr. Carver's. I've never known you to take more than five minutes to get dressed. What's up?"

"Well, there's Honey and Di, you know," Trixie answered, coloring slightly at her brother's having caught her thinking about her appearance. "They always take longer than I do."

"Oh, you *femmes!*" Mart teased, pretending to powder his nose. "Go ahead. We'll be waiting to admire the results of your cosmetology, never fear!"

When the girls finally were ready, the boys, even Mart, admitted they looked "real neat," which, of course, was the highest compliment they could have paid them. Trixie had on a sleeveless white piqué dress that enhanced her suntan. Di was in pale lavender, a color she loved because she knew it made her eyes look even more deeply purple, and Honey was wearing a flowered print. Their hair was shining, and their discreetly applied light lipstick made them look unusually pretty. It was a gay group that headed for Green Trees.

They decided to stop and see Lizzie on the way, hoping to find out if Mr. Lynch had offered her the job. As they drove up, they saw the old lady sitting on the store steps in the sun. As soon as she saw them, she got up and hurried toward the station wagon.

"I was waiting for you to drive past," she said,

a smile lighting up her wrinkled old face. "Mr. Lynch told me you'd be going out to Green Trees about this time, so I figured I'd wait for you. I guess you know why he was here."

"Yes, he said he planned to talk to you," Trixie said, "and from the way you look, I'll bet I can guess what was decided."

The Bob-Whites were amazed at the transformation in Lizzie. She was wearing a fresh housedress, and her hair was neatly combed back in a tight bun. The bright expression on her face made her seem years younger.

"Bless you, Trixie," she said. "This was your doin's, I'll be bound. I'm going to Green Trees and take care of the place while Edgar is away, and then, when he comes back, I'm going to stay for as long as he needs me." Then, somewhat hesitantly, she added, "I guess I was wrong about you Northerners. Mr. Lynch is certainly a fine gentleman!"

She was jubilant, and the Bob-Whites shared her happiness. They finally bade her good-bye, saying they were sorry they couldn't stay longer. As they drove away, Trixie, looking back, saw her standing in the middle of the road, still waving to them.

As they approached Mr. Carver's gate, they found Neil waiting for them in the driveway. His face was shining, his hair was slicked down, and he was wearing what looked to be new chinos and a madras jacket. Trixie suspected Mr. Lynch had had something to do with this transformation, but she, like the others, didn't mention his appearance, lest she embarrass him. They chatted about the horses and Mr. Lynch's plans for Rosewood as they walked toward the house. Mr. Carver was at the door waiting to greet them, and right behind him stood Miss Bates, looking absolutely resplendent in a bright red brocade gown. Her gray hair, piled high on her head, was secured by two Chinese chopsticks, stuck in at rakish angles. The sensible walking shoes she usually wore had been replaced by high-heeled satin pumps, which caused her to teeter slightly when she walked.

As they went together into the dining room, where the Lynches and Dr. Brandon had already gathered, all the Bob-Whites gave cries of delight. The room glowed with the light of many candles in the wall sconces and in several large candelabras. A bowl of talisman roses dominated the sideboard, and another low arrangement of flowers graced the center of the dining table. Place cards in silver holders directed the guests to their seats. Trixie found she was on one side of Mr. Carver at the head of the table, and Mrs. Lynch was on his right. Miss Bates sat at the opposite end, with Mr. Lynch and Jim at either side of her.

When they were all seated, Mr. Carver rang a little crystal bell, and a maid, dressed in black with a crisp white apron and cap, appeared. The first course was icy cold punch served in delicate stemmed glasses. When everyone had been served, Mr. Carver held up his hand to quiet the lively conversation around him.

"I should like," he said, raising his glass, "to propose a toast to someone whom, though I have known her only a few days, I consider to be one of the best friends I've ever had. To Trixie!"

Everyone drank and cheered while Trixie tried to hold back the tears of happiness she felt welling up in her eyes. Then Mr. Carver reached in his pocket and drew something out.

"And," he continued, "as a remembrance of your trip to Rosewood Hall, I want you to have this." He handed her the gold locket. As Trixie slowly opened the little heart and looked once again at the picture of Ruth and her husband, Mr. Carver said, "I'm sure you'll have a picture to put in the space where the secret message was."

Before she thought what she was doing, Trixie raised her head and looked down the table at Jim. No one had to guess whose picture she would choose.

Soup was followed by roast beef, cooked to just the right degree of pinkness, fluffy mashed potatoes, and peas. Mart, who was obviously enjoying every mouthful, finally could control his curiosity no longer. Looking first at Miss Bates and then at Mrs. Lynch, he said, "Excuse me if I ask a personal question, but I can't figure out how you two managed all this on such short notice."

"I'll let you in on the secret," Mrs. Lynch chuckled. "At Miss Bates's suggestion, I phoned a caterer in Washington and arranged to have everything brought down to Mr. Carver's by truck."

"Will wonders never cease!" Mart cried, attacking the roast beef again. "Three cheers for Mrs. Lynch and Miss Bates!"

"And three cheers for Mr. Carver for inviting us in the first place!" Trixie added.

As everyone was clapping, Trixie noticed Jim, who was sitting next to Neil, giving her a covert signal. Guessing at once that Neil might want to say something but was too reticent to take the initiative, Trixie said, "Neil, how about you? Have you got a special cheer, too?"

The boy pushed back his chair and stood up.

"Well, I've been thinking," he began, scratching his head self-consciously. "I'm not too good with fancy words, but I think Dr. Brandon, here, ought to get a hand. He's going to fix it so Mr. Carver gets a chance to walk again. So here's to Dr. Brandon!"

"Thank you, Neil," Alex Brandon said warmly when the room had become quiet again. "And, you know, I'm counting heavily on *you* to help us."

By the time they had finished the ovations, the table had been cleared for dessert. A hush fell over the room as the door to the kitchen opened wide. The maid came in, carrying a huge silver tray. She put it down carefully in front of Diana. On it was a birthday cake unlike any the Bob-Whites or the other guests had ever seen. It looked just like Miss Bates's rose-trimmed hat, the very one she had sworn to eat if Trixie found the secret passage!

"Happy birthday to you!" they all sang as Di took

a deep breath and blew out the candles that surrounded the crown of the hat. Then, poking an inquiring finger into the masterpiece, she burst out laughing.

"It's cake, all right, and all these roses are frosting! Oh, Mummy, Daddy!" she cried. "Thanks for a wonderful surprise!"

"You have Miss Bates to thank for the cake, my dear," Mrs. Lynch said. "It was *her* idea."

"Goodness, I had to do *something* to avoid having to eat that old straw hat!" Miss Bates laughed heartily. "Now cut it, Di, and you can all help me eat it!"

As the party finally drew to a close and good-byes were being said, Trixie moved to Mr. Carver's side.

"You know," she said, "I'd be really sad to have this trip come to an end, except that we have so much to look forward to: your coming to New York, a visit with Miss Julie to tell her all we've discovered, and maybe—" She hesitated.

"And maybe another mystery?" He finished the sentence for her.

"Who knows?" Trixie laughed. "It does seem that Honey was right when she said I attract them like a magnet attracts nails!"

Honey was right when she said I attract them like a